The Bad Seed

*A subtly sinister tale told
with humour and grace*

Maurilia Meehan

BeWrite Books
www.bewrite.net

Published internationally by BeWrite Books, UK.
32 Bryn Road South, Wigan, Lancashire, WN4 8QR.

A CIP catalogue record for this book is available from the British Library

ISBN 1-905202-12-1

Also available in eBook format.

Produced by BeWrite Books

Cover art © Catherine Acin 2005

Also by Maurilia Meehan

Performances
Fury
Adultery
The Sea People
Furie hinter den Spiegeln

Maurilia Meehan lives in Hepburn Springs in the spa district of Victoria, Australia. The mists and odd atmosphere of this region inspired her to write her fifth novel, The Bad Seed.

Her previous works have been favorably noted in many awards and have been published in Australia, France and Germany, most recently in *La Nouvelle Revue Française*. Fury was shortlisted for the prestigious Miles Franklin Award and published in Germany.

The author would like to thank Leilah Rose, Peter Templeton, Catherine Acin and Haig Becker for their magic spells, both textual and otherwise, and also Meredith Whitford. Thank you to Catherine Acin for the cover image. *The Life of The Bee* by Maurice Maeterlinck, *The Secret Life of Money* by Tad Crawford, and the many tales of El Dorado have also inspired these pages.

An extract from *The Bad Seed* appeared in *Hecate* magazine, University of Queensland, edited by the amazing Carole Ferrier.

The Bad Seed

Part One

Agatha Hock was doing autumn again. She cut it into separate words then jumbled them until a pattern emerged.

Ah, autumn again ... yesterday, I went down with Mary-Mary to pick the last dahlias ...

Agatha was gardening columnist for *Womanly You*. It should have been easy to turn out another gardening romance, as her editor called it. After all, there were only four seasons. She had only to submit, each quarter, variations on the same story, each starring Agatha Hock once more exploring the treasures of her vast estate with her cherubic daughter, Mary-Mary, assumed to be about six. (She had remained about six for several years, but no one seemed to notice.)

She did prefer autumn to any other season, partly because the days were noticeably shorter and she could thus start drinking earlier (her rule was – never before sundown). People who met her at lunch at the magazine thought, no doubt, that she was a teetotaller but Agatha, like most of us, had a side that only the moon ever saw. Agatha drank, not seriously, but consistently.

She took a sip of whisky. Still the red and yellow leaves, her daughter crunching them underfoot, the mulching, all that, were not jumping into any helpful formation. She shuffled the words again.

... at one's feet and just asking to be mulched.

Mmm. That might work.

Ever since she had submitted her first column, all contact had been by email or phone, so no one had actually seen her vast estates, which was fortunate. Because to even glimpse a garden Agatha had to leave her lime-green flat surrounded by sharp cactus and gravel, and walk down to the nature strip bordering the freeway outside. It was true that she loved gardening, what she had done with the nature strip proved it, but she enjoyed *reading* about gardening more. She knew about Vita's Sissinghurst and about Hidcote and about Edna Walling's work and the illustrations of these gardens were the inspiration for her columns.

She allowed readers to picture her, the red leaves of her maple trees fluttering down onto her as she planted her snowflakes and daffodils and grape hyacinths (for the plot line of autumn included, as well as mulch, bulbs).

As for her daughter, Mary-Mary; well, she had once had a daughter. A strange sentence that. She had once been a mother. Was she a mother still? All was unclear, since the disappearance. The truth about what had happened that night was still a dark place at the centre of her life. One she skirted around, eyes averted.

Truth of another kind was threatening Agatha at the moment, and it was this that was distracting her from her current column. Her editor had suggested a readers' competition to be announced in the next issue of *Womanly You*. A tour of Agatha's estate was to be the first prize.

Agatha had managed to put off this competition until next year, insisting the best time for her garden, her special time, would be next autumn. The editor had conceded, allowing it would give more lead-time.

'After the launch the tours could be yearly, with workshops.'

'Perhaps.'

'And they would love to meet Mary-Mary ...'

Who was, of course, Quite-Contrary, and another of the illusions on which Agatha's life was built. Mary-Mary's namesake was Mary Poppins, her real daughter's favourite book. Because she had never seen the saccharine movie version, she had been quite afraid of Mary Poppins, had nightmares about her, but had still loved reading about her.

So Agatha was now searching for some kind of cheap country place before her illusory non-garden was discovered.

She had an appointment with an estate agent for the next day. She would definitely have to go cottage garden – that was all she could possibly afford. She hoped her editor would approve.

She sighed and shuffled the words around again.

There is no time like autumn to plant bulbs in readiness for the splendour of spring.

She came to the necessary phrase about fancies turning to love, came to her usual battle to draw a not-too-cute picture of Mary-Mary in that white bonnet and carrying that little gardening trowel.

When Agatha found a cottage, perhaps up near Wombat Hill, she could then suggest a column on rescuing an old neglected garden. And then the tours could go on, the problem of earning a living neatly solved, and Mary-Mary could live with her, never seen, never ageing.

And Frank? He would come back perhaps, Frank the truthful, Frank the non-illusory, Frank, with whom she knew where she stood. This had been his attraction for her. Perhaps in a relationship two dreamers make it impossible to continue – only one is allowed.

Frank prided himself on always facing the truth and he needed to have this virtue witnessed. Not by another truth-facer who would take it for granted, but witnessed by a dreamer who would acknowledge it as a virtue. Just as two dreamers in a relationship would not feel they had the upper hand, the secret life that made them feel safe, so two truth-facers would miss having this virtue applauded.

And so she kept on dreaming that Frank would one day return and that she would find her daughter on her doorstep.

It had to be Frank, for there was definitely no sign of an incarnation of love in her life since Frank had taken off. She supposed she was still *with* him. They were definitely friends and together they had been through the horror of their daughter's disappearance. It had cemented their relationship, but at the same time they did not want to see each other for fear of being reminded of the loss.

In plant terms she saw him as a hardy perennial or perhaps a dry-climate oak, definitely of the evergreen variety, a good windbreak, a provider of wide shade. Though he would see himself more as a stringybark, perhaps, especially with his sunburnt skin in summer, more of a republican tree, trekking his way up the Great Dividing Trail, alone, leather boots, tent and all.

What was she? A plant that hated direct sunlight; maybe a hydrangea, easily drying out, needing shelter. Though, of course, nothing could grow under an oak so she was clearly, she told herself, better off without him.

In the sloping backyard jungle there is a dragon. Made of white stone, its open mouth swallows children alive. Birds sit on the curled tongue – in a blink, they disappear. Swallowed whole.

Around the dragon is a circle of thick green grass and red-capped toadstools. The blackberries that have taken over the rest of the garden dare not encroach on the dragon's territory.

On nights of the full moon spring water oozes from the dragon's mouth. Magpies as big as eagles drink the water, carolling sweetly or calling hoarsely according to their magpie moods. They drink and grow to twice the size of the other magpies in the town, these witch's magpies. They swarm over her blackberry-buried house at dawn and dusk, screeching.

Children always find a witch's house.

They dream of pinching an electric saw from an unwatched shed, hacking through that thorny jungle, just like the prince in Sleeping Beauty.

What would they find behind the thorns?

A princess asleep on a silken bed?

The blackberries are as high as the roof. A forest of thorns overgrowing the once clipped box hedge which now supports the bowers of blackberries, long tendrils reaching out, ever seeking, ever consuming, destroying native, or just weaker, strains of life. In summer it is wild with bees. In April it offers a forbidden feast of blackberries – no one is sure if the berries are sprayed by the council or not. The children eat poisoned blackberries, then lie awake at night, trying not to scratch at thorn pricks on their hands and unprotected legs, imagining every stomach rumble might bring on death and, worse, the discovery of their crime.

In winter the grey tangled thorns are laid bare. From the top of the hill they can see what lies behind the forest. Tall purple and white seed heads, cobwebs as wide as eagles' wings draping the house, which is resisting the determined, insistent trails of blackberry tapping at windows, knocking at doors.

And there is washing on a wire line on the back veranda. Grey dishcloths that may be her underwear. Crocheted rugs that may be her clothes. Neighbours believe she was there when they were children. But their own dead parents had spoken of her being there when they themselves were children.

She comes outside to feed the birds. She comes outside to put her rubbish out. But even witches have to use the correct green plastic ones and the council long ago stopped collecting her leaking paper bags, so she walks down to a room under the back veranda, places it on the pile, carefully, as if it is an offering to a god.

Ding Dong, the wicked witch is.

She hears the unseen children, throws a handful of dirt or a peg in their direction. The heart is the whole body as they scramble, stumble away through the scrub, through the dry wiry beginnings of the State Forest.

Afraid she will cast a spell.

Turn you into a.

Cook you in the.

The children who once watched from the hill grow up to be young people with jobs in newly gentrified Wombat. Jobs in what is politely called the hospitality industry. The new servant class. There is work to keep them here, and so the parents must be grateful to the trendies, though houses now can only be painted in dull heritage colours. (The witch's house was once blue, a lovely colour for a house, but you weren't allowed to use that now.)

Neighbours used to bring the witch soup, leaving it as near as they could get to the thorn-enveloped letterbox. They collected the mail, which the postman left under a stone. Nothing personal, they couldn't help noticing. Glancing.

At first they used nice crockery tureens made in China for the soup. But she never returned the lids. One had a nice pattern of a family of ducks but she said it had no lid. The same happened with the one with the sunflowers.

These stories passed from one phone to the next. The lid with the sunflowers became a set of sunflower soup bowls, the family of ducks became an antique soup tureen shaped like a duck. It was rumoured that she attended a market stall in a distant town with all her ill-gotten goods. Then it was reported that an antique tureen shaped like a duck was for sale in Main Street. No one, of course, could remember exactly whose it was by that stage. It was soon sold, anyway, for a ridiculous price to one of the weekend tourists. Lifeblood of the town. In whose honour the columbines and daffodils and lavender (above all lavender) bloomed, for whose pleasure the massage tables groaned, the hospitality workers stroked tired skin with fragrant oils, cooked and cleaned and above all, smiled.

In this town, illusion was stronger than truth. There was the problem with the water, this magic, curative spa water, on which the town floated. The council was working on it. The problem was there, under the nose of any tourist, if they would only look beyond the reliably fabricated bucolic bliss, the computer-generated dream that was each weekend.

The lake knew. The white weatherboard, wide verandaed hotel on the lake knew and the Devonshire teahouses knew. But no one would admit it. Or the illusion that brought prosperity, or the closest the locals would get to it, would evaporate as surely as the Sunday market vanished into clouds on winter mornings.

Wombat was one and a half hours from Melbourne, and poverty and scratching for a living after the gold rush boom had made sure the town had remained as picturesque as the city folk liked their romantic getaways to be. And, of course, it was magic. It was the only spa town in the Southern Hemisphere. The Swiss-Italians (who came from a country called Swissitalia, according to eighty-seven per cent of the local primary school children) knew about spas, of course. Their curative properties. Their magic. These people had planted pines and oaks and yews in the mountain air, giving it a European feel that was difficult to manage at lower altitudes. Here, the picture book gardens of Sissinghurst and Hidcote could grow; down in the city and the flat wheat lands that surrounded this botanical heaven, the shortage of water meant natives reigned.

And even the most patriotic Australian needs a break from eucalypts.

So, floating on underground waters as the town was, it was odd that that a request for water at a cafe table would be greeted with a forced smile.

'Which brand?'

'Oh, just the local spa water.'

'We only sell bottled and we have to charge.'

By now the customer was peeved.

'I'm sorry health regulations do not permit ...'

And so a brand of water he could buy in the city, or in Europe, was plonked on the table.

In the stores around the nation, waters from Wombat Spring are bottled. And sold clear, clean and with the sulphur flavour filtered out. But here, in the town, the water from the springs is yellowish to brown, varies in effervescence, differed in taste from pump to pump. These waters were not aesthetically pleasing enough to be served at table.

The visitors want to sleep late, be served a breakfast of sausages and bacon or Special K (depending on how abandoned their weekend is). Don a pair of two hundred and fifty dollar Italian walking boots and amble a few hundred metres to one of the pumps dotting the oak and pine parks that hide the scraggy gum forests from view. Pretend they are in Italy or France. Reminisce about their last trip overseas, which, with the dreadful current exchange rate and the crash of the dotcoms, was inevitably a long time ago.

They do not know about the witch's house behind the forest of thorns.

For a while, the neighbours stopped the soup-runs. To see what would happen.

She seemed to get even thinner. She was like some ancient half-wrapped mummy, her arms and legs bent permanently at the knees and elbows, which gave her a horror-movie lurch when she walked. Yellow skin and feverish apple-red cheeks.

So they resumed the soup-runs, only this time it was plastic ice-cream buckets. Neapolitan, chocolate crunch, honeycomb, Diet-Rite. Who cared if she gave *those* lids back or not?

Vegetable soup, tomato soup, they cooked a bit extra and were conscious of being generous. Proud of owning the country ways that were extolled in margarine and coffee ads on TV. Not mean like city folk, those black-clad thin ones who invaded the town on weekends in their sports cars.

She had been there longer than anyone in the whole street.

She had arrived before time.

One day, the ice-cream bucket – was it vegetable with barley that day? – was left uneaten on the front door mat. Flies buzzed. A black cat was seen scratching at the lid. That was too much. The cook reclaimed it. There was a note attached.

I am tired of soup.

The nerve. And after all the trouble. Ungrateful.

Well, how would she survive? She could just shrivel up and keel over ...

But the next day *Meals on Wheels* pulled up. A big tray of foil-covered dishes. You could smell the custard and stewed apple. A knock on the door. No trouble. That went on for a month or so. Nicer smelling meals than before. But everyone hates a fussy beggar, and people stopped caring about the witch.

The parents stopped reprimanding the children when they sang. *Ding-Dong!*

Then *Meals on Wheels* stopped.

Neighbours watched then as the blackberries took over the steep steps which climbed to the front door, the rubbish mounted like fortifications at the back (the stink!), and as the junk mail became coloured mounds of confetti on the ground around the letterbox.

How do witches die?

For reference we could look at how Wendy in the *Wizard of Oz* killed the Wicked Witch of the West. They do burn, of course, if you can find an oven big enough – perhaps a pizza oven in an Italian restaurant would do. Some of the old Swiss-Italian hotels in Wombat might have one big enough. Still, you would have to get her to have a meal out with you, and would the restaurateur exercise the *we reserve the right to ...?* Hansel and Gretel had an unfair advantage, living as they did in home-baking days.

You can't drown them, of course; the whole Inquisition was based on that.

So how did this witch die?

Slowly, and in pain.

The coroner saw that her body was deformed at the joints, which were more or less fixed in a flexed position. This gave her the odd hobbling way of walking that the children knew marked her as a witch. The small joints of the hands and feet were also affected and the lower jaw and the skull just in front of the ear and the sterno-clavicular joint between the collarbone and the top of the breastbone also showed signs of disease. She would have told her doctor, if she had had one, that her joints were swollen, stiff and painful. There were small nodules under the skin, and the tissue around the joints was thickened. Movement would have been increasingly difficult as the deformity developed.

'Cortisone,' muttered his friend the doctor. 'Cortisone could have fixed her.'

'And physiotherapy. It is important to maintain movement in such cases.'

The two men, over the woman's corpse, spoke accusingly of the neighbours.

The electricity company eventually sent in a grader to clear the way to the meter, next to the front door. Ripping the thorn brambles out by their roots, pushing them back so they lay on their brothers, clearing a rough way to the door, itself threatened with home invasion by the inquisitive, creeping, scouting tendrils sent out by the master plant, whose roots remained under secret cover.

The neighbours heard the woman was found in noxious fumes of vomit and diarrhoea, collapsed on the floor of her kitchen. They heard her food shelves were empty. There was nothing in the house to eat.

They knew they were not to blame. They knew they had done all they could. Because their questions might single them out for blame, they could not ask what they really wanted to know.

What was in the little leather first-aid case, an antique by the look of it, which was carried away on top of the white sheet covering the stretcher?

The children knew what was in the case. Spells. An old spell-kit, two thousand years old. They would die if they touched it.

They waited out of sight until the body was in the ambulance. Then they ran after it, not caring about being covered in dust.

Ding Dong the witch is dead.
The wicked witch is dead.

And the parents went inside their houses and talked about how much the witch's property might be worth.

The town was, in general, pretty overvalued, they knew. It was close to Melbourne, but a bit far to commute daily. And of course the cell-phones dropped out, it was the dark ages up here. And in winter it was, let's face it, bloody cold, bloody rainy and bloody foggy. The old felt it in their bones, and for that reason city folk did not buy here to retire.

So the town was destined to remain picturesquely impoverished. Houses that should have been pulled down and replaced by nice brick veneers long ago were instead tarted up for sale to city types. If you were careful and stuck to the heritage colours and pulled out the practical gas fire and put in a wood burning one, and kept the garden in the cottage style, all primroses and granny bonnets, a city cat would pay a ridiculous amount for a tumbledown fibro shack. Usually in summer. By winter, they discovered that the roof leaked, that open fires do not heat a house and that there was borer in the floor. The neighbours assumed these three things about the house next door. So did the town's only estate agent. My God, who would buy that dump? Still, if you had the money, with property values the way they were, it would be worth cleaning it up. They fantasised about buying it, pulling down the house, replacing it with a double-garage, another clothesline, an outdoor BBQ area or a pergola.

And the bag of spells?

Actually, it was a leather first aid kit with an old metal zip. Inside was a large old-fashioned syringe and some vials of gold dust and a metal medicine glass with etched measurements. The deceased, it seemed, had injected herself with gold dust. And had drunk it from the medicine glass, swilled in water. This was not as strange a habit to a doctor as it would have appeared to the neighbours.

Gold has certain known curative properties. It was once used to treat tuberculosis. It is still sometimes used for the treatment of rheumatoid arthritis, from which this woman obviously suffered. The mode of action of gold on rheumatoid arthritis is still not understood.

Of course, highly refined gold salts were needed. Not the gold dust the deceased had used, however finely she had ground it. The deceased, self-educated in these matters, possessed a library on all aspects of gold, including its curative properties, and had attempted to treat herself.

However, she had failed to note that gold should not be used when the patient suffered from any disease of the liver or the kidneys, or the skin. In these cases, gold is liable to give rise to toxic effects that include generalised skin reactions, damage to the kidneys leading to the passing of blood and albumin in the urine and the diminution of white cells in the blood. Gold may prove poisonous to the liver.

And, explaining the state in which she was found, it may produce jaundice, vomiting and diarrhoea.

People exist, of course, long after they have died. Kept alive in the minds of those who loved or hated them, even in the minds of those they merely irritated, or who were indifferent to them. But they are preserved at different ages, with gaps in between.

Agatha still had her daughter, Daphne, age three, listening to *Sleeping Beauty*. Daphne is always wearing a fuzzy lemon, blue and pink striped jumper Agatha had knitted.

'Gelati colours,' she said, and called it her ice-cream jumper.

Before this age, the dawn of literacy, there was no picture unless she deliberately called it up. A breech birth and three years of sleep deprivation were not willingly remembered.

Then her memory fast-forwarded to shopping at the supermarket together, cheese sticks or chips at the checkout.

Brown sugar from the bowl.

Agatha's own mother being shocked when they visited and Daphne had asked what *the white stuff* was in the bowl on the table.

'My God, doesn't the poor child know what sugar is?'

And now her own mother was gone, what did Agatha remember of her?

The soft look in her eyes when her mother's young doctor appeared – do women never stop falling in love with the most unsuitable boys? Soft eyes that had not looked at her like that, ever since Agatha had *gone off the rails*. Led astray by studying.

University is for plain girls, Agatha, for girls who can't find husbands.

She had almost not found Frank.

But it seemed to Agatha that uni was indeed a place for girls to find husbands. It was just that while they were all running after law and med students, she was away with the plays of Shakespeare. Even more uselessly, her special area of research was The Flowers of Shakespeare.

This got her, predictably enough, a job at the post office.

Shakespeare's Flowers had been as close as she had got to studying horticulture, and yet Agatha was now a gardening writer.

She had approached gardening initially through Shakespeare, broadening out to include Vita *et al*. It was better than working at the post office. In their lime-green flat she had no garden, which was why she had taken over the nature strip. Neighbouring tenants did not complain – it meant they didn't have to mow it.

On the nature strip ducks swam in a chipped enamel bathtub with lion-claw feet. They lived luxuriously on fat snails and grubs. The rooster vented his anger on passing cars, which swerved to dodge him. According to season there were waist-high explosions of rampant silver beet, giant rhubarb or ambitious young corn and tomatoes. Each plant was thriving on a mulch of last year's bolted parsley and withered pumpkin leaves, and all were bordered by lavender, rosemary and self-seeded rocket.

Neighbours mowed their green-jube nature strips bordering Agatha's garden and did not report her to the local council. Inspectors were turned away with filched handfuls of strawberries or beet depending on the season. Owners of these neat emerald strips turned a blind eye. They could sneak out after dark in their slippers and steal a few nice garlic chives, or a twig of rosemary for the roast. Amazing, how each plant Agatha grew *self-seeded* in the backyards of the whole street. No one knew that Agatha, whom they saw squatting in her jungle using green string to tie new *grosse lisse* tomatoes to a triangle frame made of rusted iron bedsteads, had a secret life. In this other life, she was not a hippy green-thumb, desperate for a patch of earth. The readers of *Womanly You* would, in fact, have been shocked to see her reduced to this penury.

To them she is Agatha Hock, writing for them each month from her five-acre garden, from her Arts and Crafts house with its thatched roof, where she lives with the white-bonneted Mary-Mary, and is strangely silent about her husband.

In her column, *The Happy Hock*, she eternally roams her chamomile lawn overhung by wisteria, holding a wicker basket and garden shears, deadheading roses, picking the herbs for the omelettes made from eggs her colour toned chooks supply. She wears a *Womanly You* gardening outfit (denim overalls with daisy borders, also shirts, clogs etc, same design, top quality, available by mail order only from *Womanly You*).

They would not recognise this Agatha in her saffron skirt with its border of garden dirt. Her hand-knitted lavender jumper collects the smell of the tomatoes in its fibres. She breathes in this essence of tomato, runs a thin brown hand over the young green leaves, the budding yellow flowers. She moves towards the oversize spinach. A neighbour's ginger cat pads out from under its shelter. Agatha sniffs the soil, frowns, hisses at the cat, which darts away from her.

She picks a handful of spinach, some parsley and spring onions, then, using her skirt as a basket, collects three chook eggs and two duck eggs from under the shelter of the bean canopy – a favourite nesting spot – and walking along the baby's tears path to the front door, removes her old clogs.

Who would buy such a dump?

The neighbours would have been surprised to know that they were already familiar with the future *vendee*. Knew her name from their monthly copies of *Womanly You*. Agatha Hock reminded her readers, according to the seasons, to mulch, water, sow and prune. She wrote about friable soil in a fresh way, about the importance of mulching in ever more insistent tones. Her readers, including those wondering about the future of the witch's house, would have thought hers a nice little job to have, planting her daffodils with the maple leaves falling down around her.

They would not have dreamed that Agatha was not content. Daphne's disappearance weighed on her even after five years. She had no garden of her own. And she was about to lose her job.

While they were reading her column she was daydreaming that she was a detective storywriter. She would write a book in which a

Miss Marple character, who she would wittily name Miss Maple, visits Australia, and solves Daphne's disappearance. The novel would have a murder in it, the murder of whoever abducted her daughter. She knew now the desire to commit that murderous pleasure.

Agatha was a good name, after all, for a crime writer, having been carried by the best one, though her mother had not named her after Agatha Christie, but after the agapanthus plant, that hardy immigrant from South Africa.

'Why did you call me that?'

'Because I hate the damn things,' her mother had replied. 'Always springing up where they're not wanted and dash hard to get rid of once they're there.'

Agatha was the eleventh child.

She supposed her mother had tried to abort her.

You may have seen Agatha in the old days at the city GPO, that high-ceilinged, glass-roofed monument to the dying days of the letter. Agatha Hock had been one of the counter staff. Her queue was always the longest, but not because she was the slowest. The opposite was true. Her sharp over-rapid movements as she gave you stamp booklets, slammed the postmark down onto your letters, weighed your parcels, had made her famous.

'Have you seen …?'

'You know that really quick woman at the GPO?'

There was a rumour started that she was a new kind of automated experiment – a robot, not a woman at all. There was, after all, no eye contact, the movements were so jerky, she only ever spoke to answer specific information. Prices. Times to reach destination. You could program a robot for that.

There were others who believed that she was blind. Not that she wore dark glasses, but she never looked at you. The other workers seemed to move in slow motion on each side of her, and the queue was silent in respectful admiration of her as they waited, as if in a church.

It was, some whispered, a form of manic or obsessive compulsive behaviour. They recognised it from the pages of the glossy magazine lift-out in the weekend paper. They had done the test to see to what degree they had it themselves. Did it stop at counting the slats of Venetian blinds? The number of shelves in desks in offices where they worked? At least they were not as bad as this woman. If they were lucky they saw her pull out the damp sponge she was famous for and wipe clean the area of the counter in front of her with *Windex*.

Of course, in her job where routine and order and counting were vital, her affliction was a definite employment advantage. Efficiency, that's what counted now, and an obsessive compulsive certainly had that. It could be seen as an adaptive strategy to current employment culture, so perhaps it was wrong to treat it? An advantage, this anxiety disorder, this inward turning of the fight-or-flight response.

After all. Look at the A4 poster on the wall inviting workers to attend a seminar called *Making Stress Work for You.*

Something in her life must have driven her to cope with her pain in this way, but no one knew what it was.

She was never away, never once late, but on the other hand, never showed any interest in moving to a more interesting position. A perfect worker, content, it seemed, to stay selling stamps in her truly magnificent style until she was sixty-five. Management secretly believed such a worker must be mad, and so a pre-emptive strike was made against her. She was retrenched because the managers feared a stress payout.

At her farewell party, because she was always wiping her section of the counter, because she always liked things neat and clean, they gave her industrial strength cleaner (wet and dry), cartons of cleaning products from *Half-Case Warehouse* and a dozen pairs of rubber gloves.

She smiled, said thank you, but did not make a speech. She did not seem as upset as they thought she should be about losing her job. Parties for the retrenched were always awkward. What was there to celebrate? People left early, pleading other commitments.

They did not know she had just been offered a contract as *The Happy Hock*. They did not know that she was the mother (identity suppressed by newspapers in a surprising display of restraint) of the *Milk Bar Girl*.

The first thing Agatha had noticed about being home every day in the lime-green flat with Frank (who had stopped work right after the disappearance) was that very soon their lives centred around food. Breakfast together could last for two hours. There was a poem, wasn't there, about *endless cups of tea?*

He read his bushwalking books and she worked her way through gardening books, piles of them from the library, pinching ideas for her column. Never any newspapers, of course, since Daphne's disappearance.

They developed a routine. Porridge for breakfast, reading and library, whisky at five o'clock, dinner at six thirty. After dinner, they both listened to Karl Haas present his music program at seven. Not the news.

They could no longer tolerate the news.

That had been before Frank had left to do his Great Dividing Trail Walk. Alone. She had thought all his bushwalking books had been fantasy but he had been preparing for his departure all that time.

And now Agatha Hock, prospective real estate client, was walking the streets of Wombat, looking for property. She was one of the city folk who loved Wombat and had often made day trips there with Frank. She loved the grape hyacinths in the main street gutters in September, she loved the coolness of the oak-lined lake in summer, the red and yellow hands that floated down in autumn, and the humble nudity of the trees in winter.

Agatha knew this town well.

She observed the layer of semi-permanent artistic types with knitted beanies against the cold mountain air (the area was famous for the magic mushroom harvests in the mountain forests in April). She saw the gay enclave, crafty vegans and the Europeans escaping the coming catastrophe that would bring death to all save those who lived above the tidal wave's reach.

She watched the youth of the town, smoking, gathered around the fish and chip shop on social security days, picking over the op-shops for second-hand black lingerie or platform shoes, jeans and T-shirts with slogans. They in turn watched the perfectly made up women, the men with their sports cars, the gay couples who swanned in and out of the town.

The locals didn't understand why the tourists came.

'I mean, I know it's a pretty little town, but why do they keep coming back?'

And by the end of each weekend, Sunday at five o'clock, to be precise, the smiles of the owners of the cafés, of the antique boutiques and of the herbal remedies shops were fading. Except, perhaps, for the gentle folk of *The Dragon's Den*, wrapped up in some faded leather bound edition of *The Witch's Almanac* or talking about the best guide to Crowley's *Tarot* with a ring-nosed woolly clad urchin – or with Agatha about the Flowers of Shakespeare.

And the second-hand bookshops in the town could not be faulted.

The careful elegance of the two story shop, and the roaring fire of the one by the lake – we will forget that the lake was made by drowning the Chinese market gardens that served the gold-miners, that the site was, well, of course, highly suitable for a lake, but also, well, a convenient way to get rid of the Orientals – they both were second-hand bookshops that the city visitors liked to call *world-class*.

She was emerging now from the re-developed cream and maroon spa complex into the European halo of trees, fresh from her *Total Indulgence Package*. New Age music, incense and a wholesome young masseur clad in white hospital gear, trained in discreetly turning over naked clients like Agatha, had stroked her unloved skin. Around her floated clouds of valerian. He had warned her not to drive far after this treatment. She would fall asleep at the wheel, just like in the road safety ad, just like *Sleeping Beauty*.

Agatha Hock knew to avoid the rusty little hand-pumps directly outside the spa building, which delivered up only brown, sulphurous, flat bubbles. She saved her empty water bottle for another spring, a little further away, a real drink of the gods. Slightly effervescent, cold, from the heart of the continent. Alone, she moved past the smiling couples and tried not to look at them. It was worse, of course, when she saw children, especially girls around Daphne's age. Or the age she would have been if ...

But Wombat was a honeymooner's place, not many children except for the school holidays. So, collar turned up against the cold, all bathed, scented, and massaged, she headed back to her waiting car. She was just another one of those trailing clouds of valerian or jasmine, who would emerge a few minutes later into the main street.

On her way to the Devonshire tea tables, where she would hesitate between lavender scones and plain, she stood respectfully before that modern shrine, the real estate agent's window. Here young couples adored and offered hopeful prayers, shrewder ones whispered to each other about margin calls, and locals compared their own houses with the phenomenal prices being offered for something similar (well, fairly – except for a lick of paint, the gas fire and the decking they hadn't built yet and maybe the stumps).

And then she saw the witch's house.

Rare opportunity!

Cute secluded old world charm of cosy miner's cottage with original features can be yours. Established garden, orchard at rear on large sloping block.

On either side of her, people gazed up at this and other photos.

From his desk inside, the estate agent could now lip-read a certain phrase they all mouthed.

You could be in Europe here ...

This was high praise, he knew, and usually referred to an oak tree in the yard, a fine rose trellis, or a hedge of lavender. He wished he had twenty dollars for every time someone had sighed in front of his agent's windows, *Yes, you could be.*

He noticed Agatha looking at the witch's house. He knew it was a great photo, very creative. Had to be. From the photo, you could see that the grader had been recently busy. Not a sign of blackberry from this carefully chosen angle (though it would already be silently regenerating, reconnoitering for its next attack) and the house stood open to the sun, revealed (sort of) for the first time in over a hundred years. They had clipped back the box hedges that had hidden most of the house. And it certainly sounded charming.

Inside, the agent told her it would not last at that price. He'd had an offer already; she'd have to decide that afternoon.

It was dusk by the time they pulled up outside it, and Agatha Hock, flat-dwelling gardener, was overwhelmed by the size of the land, saw a vision of a vast garden splendid (dusk was kind to the waiting blackberries) in which she would establish her *Womanly You* tours – and she was suddenly inspired by a *garden concept* that she knew her editor would love.

The agent, for some reason, did not have a key to go inside, but invited her to look through the windows, on which blackberry tendrils were tapping.

'A little work needed, but for that price ...' he muttered, as they stumbled along the narrow, recently cleared path. She almost fell over the impatient blackberry roots, already resprouting, green and intractable, slashed back but not defeated. The windows were covered with faded cloth hanging from rusty nails. The agent, anxious to avert her eyes from closer inspection, pointed to a rectangular object at her feet.

'That's original too,' he said.

It was an old wooden sign, the paint peeling off. The grader must have knocked it down and left it there. Blue and cream writing stood out in the half-light.

Agatha Springs

The smallest hotel in the world.

That clinched this rather emotive sale. Unfortunately, Agatha Hock, astute investor, was not present, and Agatha Hock, canny renovator, was definitely out. That left only Agatha Hock, believer in signs, to have her way unopposed.

She gazed at the wooden sign again.

Agatha Springs ...

The agent saw he was in luck. He hit her with his best line. 'You know, Agatha, when you've been in this business as long as I have, you know that some things were just *meant* to be.' He nodded wisely at his own remark.

And he knew from her eyes that here was another city cat signed up for a tumbledown shack that the grader should have razed.

'Ideal for B&B, walk to spa, overlooking state forest, adjacent old gold diggings. Renovator's delight or weekend retreat. Restore *The Smallest Hotel in the World* ...' he prattled.

Just to be sure.

Her editor was not enthralled with Agatha's garden concept. 'A bit highbrow for us, don't you think?'

Still, Agatha managed to get more time before the Open Garden of Agatha Hock was announced as a prize, or, worse, as an annual event. She convinced her editor that she was going to shift to the country and establish a completely new garden, a cottage garden that would *feature all the flowers mentioned in Shakespeare.* What a brainwave, this concept. They could call the tour *Shakespeare's Garden.*

'I'm not over the moon about it. I'll get sales to look at it ...'

'But – '

'I'll get back to you.'

Yet it was a brainwave, reflected Agatha. For, focusing as it would on questions about literature, the answers to which could be found in books, her relative inexperience as a *real* gardener could remain a secret. Nicely diverted as guests would be by her specialist knowledge – that Shakespeare's *woodbine* was just honeysuckle, for example – her generalist knowledge would be assumed. No one would test her about Ph values in soil, the benefits of calcium or levels of nitrogen needed by camellias.

And I serve the fairy queen
to dew her orbs upon the green.
The cowslips tall her pensioners be ...
I must go seek some dewdrops here,

And hand a pearl in every cowslip's ear.

She would reproduce the poetry, on antiqued parchment perhaps, aware, as a businesswoman, that there would be no copyright to pay. There would be illustrations of cowslips, heart's-ease. Shakespeare, she knew, had named over one hundred and eighty plants. Daffodils, of course, she knew well, so she could feature *A Winter's Tale:*

When daffodils begin to peer,
With heigh, the doxy o'er the dale,
Why then comes in the sweet o' the year,
For the red blood reigns in the water pale.

It was a great business plan, she believed, charmingly original but relatively straightforward. The magazine had at least given her time to work on it, and she was sure sales would love it. *Womanly You* could afford to move a bit up-market.

There's rosemary, that's for remembrance,
And there pansies, that's for thoughts,
Fennel, columbines, rue, daisy, violets.

This plan arose from Agatha Hock, mistress of the grand dream. She saw *Shakespeare's Garden*, as clearly as if it were already there.

I know a bank where the wild thyme blows,
Where oxlips and the nodding violet grows:
Quite over-canopied with luscious woodbine,
With sweet musk roses and with eglantine.

She knew woodbine was honeysuckle, and eglantine was *Rosa eglanteria*, a vigorous grower to two metres, as her gardening column might advise. Her printed sheets on how to grow the plants, and even seedlings to buy, would be a fine parallel income for her, for *Womanly You.*

Perhaps she would keep bees here, as many Tudor gardens had kept beehives, though she was too afraid of them. She fantasised about feeding them on blue hyssop, *Hyssopus officinalis*, with its spikes of deep blue flowers which, she had read, bees loved. She would have the plant on show and include cooking recipes using minty hyssop leaves in casseroles. So many of Shakespeare's plants were edible anyway – sweet marjoram, thyme, chamomile, rosemary, lemon balm, spearmint. Even pinks, the ancestors of modern carnations, which he called gillyflowers, could be used in mulled wine. Pied daisies were common English lawn daisies, cuckoo-bud was *Lychnis flos-cuculi*, and his *lady smocks all silver white* were meadowcress, or *Cardamine pratensis*. Then there were lavenders, snowdrops, lad's love, bluebells and love-in-idleness, or heart's-ease.

Yet mark'd I where the bolt of Cupid fell,
It fell upon a little western flower,
Before milk-white; now purple with love's wound,
And maidens call it, Love-in-idleness.

Waiting for settlement, back in the lime-green flat, Agatha's nightmare returned as it did every night.

The waiting. The phone calls that proved to be false hopes. The refusal to believe that the doorbell was not Daphne. Every time. Every minute.

Frank and Agatha had sat opposite each other in the lounge room, after Karl Haas, silent. Every night. They knew they were both thinking the same thoughts.

What if she was abducted?

Cut up.

Locked in a basement.

Raped.

Sold.

Killed.

Drugged.

At first they had watched the news, looking for clues. They watched street kids, suicides, AIDS deaths and heroin overdoses. They did not sleep.

Neither of them went out much in case the phone rang. Agatha emailed her columns regularly. Frank was drawing on all the holiday and sick leave he had carefully built up.

Sometimes, when she could no longer sit in the same room with him, she sat outside on the porch. But soon Frank would call out to her from the deep rest of his armchair, his padded nest, worn to his shape. She would glance at her watch before answering him, for two reasons. The first was to check how long she had been sitting on the back porch, gazing at the last of the red leaves clinging precariously to the branches of the Japanese maple. It was always the last to lose its leaves as winter approached. The second reason she looked at her watch was to know what he would want, because they lived their lives by the clock now, trying to maintain a pattern in their lives. As it was five o'clock, they would be having a whisky, with two ice cubes each, in the crested free glasses that came with a boxed bottle he bought for himself each birthday. Two weeks ago he had turned forty-five, so the bottle was not quite empty. It was his turn to pour the gold into the glasses, sparkling liquid over two neat glaciers.

She came back into the overheated room and they drank in silence together.

Soon it would be six o'clock. That was time to prepare dinner, but they would sit there, with the whisky, till then.

They could no longer watch TV. Every horror movie seemed to feature a tortured young girl.

You will perhaps remember the newspaper reports. The blue rain jacket, very flimsy, for it had been just a summer shower. The police had made Agatha pick out a similar one at K-Mart. It was photographed. Did you see the photo of the store dummy in the newspaper, wearing it?

It had no face.

You will perhaps remember the headlines.

CHILD MISSING.

CHILD SIGHTED WITH MAN ...

BLUE VAN

And so on, until

HOPE LOST FOR MILKBAR GIRL.

That was what they called her in the end. *The Milkbar Girl.*

In Wombat, there would be space.

Agatha would have her own driveway, there would be no parking problem. In the city, Agatha and Frank had the car problem. They lived one block from a busy shopping street and cars crawled around their street, all looking for the perfect park. As soon as she moved the car from its parking spot under the gum tree, somebody else would take it. As soon as she drove away, she could always see a car behind her, ready to zoom into her spot.

Frank didn't like driving. He used to commute by train to the city, using the time to work out intricate bushwalking trips he would, when they retired, go on with her. He knew where they would walk together. Cradle Mountain. Cinque Terre. The Cevennes, the area of R.L. Stevenson's *Travels with my Donkey.*

'Which one of us would be the donkey?' she asked.

But he loved R.L. Stevenson, and collected different editions of *Treasure Island* and *Dr Jekyll and Mr Hyde,* which sat on the mantelpiece over the gas fire.

He had taken them with him.

After about a year, Frank and Agatha had started fighting about Daphne's room. Agatha was keeping it just as it had been that night. Her pyjamas were folded on the pillow, ready for her to return. Frank said it was gruesome, that they should put her things away, get on with life. Frank nagged her to pack it all up. He said it was like living with a coffin in the house. Frank was, after all, a truth-facer.

But what if Daphne returned at eleven one night and there was no room for her?

They stopped talking about it.

But soon he announced that he was heading off alone on the bushwalk. He had said it was for the weekend. It turned out to be The Great Dividing Trail they had planned to do together, when they retired. He let her know by email that he would be back in six months.

He is still not back, though the emails still come regularly. They are friends.

And so Agatha wanders alone in Wombat, soon to be her new home. In particular, she haunts the bookshop by the lake. It is in an original cottage, heated by an open fire, and has an excellent gardening section, but other books too, deliciously time-consuming. There is even an Australian section, more common now that foreigners seem to expect it. Ah, the foreign tourists, they are so pleased by Wombat, and are beginning to arrive now in their busloads. There is also a coffee shop on the lake, right opposite the bookshop.

Heaven, no?

Hell, thought Agatha.

In the daylight, of course, she had seen her mistake. As soon as she had stepped up the steep path onto the veranda, she almost put her foot through the floorboards. She ran her hand over the outside wall, the grey, worn weatherboards, bare of all paint, and noted the holes in the spouting. The glass in the windows was caked with brown dust.

But when she opened the door, a gentle yellow light fell on the slow combustion cooker in the kitchen and on the worn wooden table was a vase of fresh dahlias, a teapot shaped like a cottage and two teacups. As if someone had been expecting her. An attempt had been made to clean the place up, and there was a basket of chopped wood near the cooker.

In short, it looked as if the previous owner had just stepped out for a few minutes and would return at any moment. Next to the hurricane lamp on the mantelpiece she saw candles and matches. She suddenly wondered if there was electricity, and she searched around for plugs. There were several of the old two-hole variety, but of course it wasn't connected in her name yet.

In the bedroom off the kitchen, she could make out wallpaper made of magazine pictures, and quilts folded back on an iron bed. On the other side of the kitchen was the bathroom from which came a damp, rotting, earthy smell. Next to a clean claw-foot bath was a chip heater, and there was a boarded-up door to the right. The bare wooden floor was rotten with damp. She would have to pull up the floorboards. Careful not to put her foot through the boards again, she took a few steps over to the tap and turned it on. Clear running water, unexpectedly strong pressure.

She turned it off, went down the dark hallway.

The spare room off this musty corridor appeared not to have been used for years. There was another iron bed, a dressing table with a pitcher and ewer with a pattern of violets. Rotting cloth blocked out the sunlight. She would keep the door to this room shut, for the meantime, and get her living area in order.

Back in the kitchen, giving in to the demands of the house, she stoked the fire up, put an old enamel kettle on the stove, lit the lamp and started to unpack. It had taken four huge boxes to pack up the shrine she had made of her daughter's room in their flat in the city.

Sooner than she had intended, she was pulling down the rotting hessian that covered the windows and darkened the room, then sitting back on the dusty bed, amazed at what was revealed.

Leadlight windows around the three walls provided wide views of the back yard that rose steeply up to the State Forest. There seemed to be a kind of green clearing that the blackberries had spared. She wiped the dust from the windows, and discovered that every window was decorated with a stained glass pattern of a mermaid sitting by a pool.

But what was the smell? The rotting smell from the bathroom was stronger here. There was a boarded-up door, she noticed, which must lead into it. The rest of the house was a crumbling ruin, but something seemed to have preserved this room. The agent could not have known what lay behind the rotting hessian, had not wanted to let her approach the smell. She could make out a poster on the wall, faded but intact.

The Smallest Hotel in The World.

She would frame it and bring it into the kitchen.

Daphne's unpacking would soon be finished.

The change of house had enabled her to compromise, to pack it all up, to store it, without throwing it away. Perhaps Frank had been right. Daphne's ghost seemed less present now that it was all packed away into the spare room in Wombat.

Wanting to listen to Daphne's voice again, she searched for that answering machine with that tape in it, but was puzzled to find it nowhere. Where had she packed it?

She had listened to that tape over and over. To hear her daughter's voice. To listen for clues. If she pulled the tape out of the machine, turned it back by hand, she could hear months of messages. She had listened to every call her daughter had made or received before the disappearance. Every male voice asking for her. She had studied the police messages, the scraps of info, the checking up.

The photo you gave us shows her with long hair but you said she has short dark hair now, could you ring back?

Have you got one showing her eyes are blue?

We need a clearer picture, can you call back?

Sorry to trouble you, but just checking the details again. Weight fifty kilos, age thirteen, hair short curly dark, blue eyes, freckles on nose and a tattoo of a mermaid near her belly button ...'

The argument about that mermaid. If she could have her back she could have as many tattoos as she liked. That had been why they were fighting, the day she disappeared. That delicate mermaid, well etched, next to her belly button. But all the parents saw was their baby's skin, bleeding. Christmas Eve and she'd gone out with a friend and done that to herself. Now it seemed so petty to fight over a mermaid tattoo.

Over and over she had listened to the tape – Daphne asking to be picked up, saying she would be late, a man with a deep voice, educated, asking her to ring him, then the police, always the police descriptions, until Frank had ripped the machine out of the wall and put it in the bag for the op-shop, saying that it was driving both of them mad.

She worked slowly; she was methodical. She knew what in was each box. First were the still wrapped Christmas presents. Then the fairy-doll, her dress tattered from sleeping for years in the lost girl's arms. Her wings were a little yellow. Then the pillow from the bed. It was printed with cartoon characters, Mickey and Minnie. Another box was a collection of cartoon figurines she had lined up on her shelves. In the next box were clothes, folded away in neat plastic bags, clothes even Agatha knew were now outdated. A pile of pop magazines from the nineties. Cheap make-up, scribbled pages from diaries, dried up bottles of nail-polish, a few pairs of shoes, the silver Doc Marten's they had gone out to buy her, when it was too late.

Better to keep it all. Daphne could throw it all out herself if she wanted to when she came back. But she would know that Agatha loved her, because she had kept it all.

The last box held schoolbooks, assignments, a school bag and pens and pencils. Notes to other kids in class. The police had seen it all. It had revealed nothing about who the man in the blue van might have been …

Last seen at the milkbar, talking to a man in a blue van …

There were her tap-shoes too. They had been the cause of another fight the night before she disappeared. She had wanted the silver Doc Marten's – two hundred and fifty dollars – not tap-shoes. She was a good dancer at school concerts.

'I don't like tap-dancing any more. Everyone else has Docs.'

She had sulked. They were already angry with her over the tattoo. They sulked too.

'You'll be sorry. I'll get them. I know someone who'll …'

'We've already bought the Christmas presents …'

'I don't want anything except Docs …'

Now all that short life was compressed into this little spare room in Wombat.

Part Two

Magdala took another drag on her herbal cigarette and flicked off her voice-recorder. She had given up smoking tobacco years ago, but still relaxed with these herbal ones, so tightly rolled that she told herself they were good for her because they exercised the jaw muscles.

Around her on the floor, on every surface, lay books, photocopies, pages, notes marked up with highlighter – the blue was for water references, the yellow for fish.

She was sitting in an armchair in the sunroom, looking out through a picture window into a water-garden. Three levels of waterfalls, Japanese grasses, and in the centre a figurine of a water-goddess from whose fingertips, the *pièce de resistance*, flowed eight fine streams of water into the highest pond.

She called out to an invisible other, 'I didn't know there was a spa in Australia.'

Silence.

'Did *you*?'

No reply save for the impatient rattle of a newspaper from the next room. She spoke louder. 'I thought we'd been to them all – but now that would be splendid. A spa with the water from the Southern Hemisphere …'

A man in his fifties, dressed in cords and a soft mohair jumper he had knitted himself, appeared at the sunroom door. He moved his glasses further back onto the bridge of his nose. In his hand was a newspaper, folded into four, with current rates of exchange marked up in blue biro.

'I thought after Vichy you said you were feeling better.'

'Better, but not splendid,' she snapped. 'I'll have to try it. I'm sure it would cure me.'

He restrained himself. It was not that she wasn't ill – she definitely had arthritis, and some kind of fainting spells were undeniable, and she could have told you of ten concurrent afflictions. It was just that he wasn't sure which one was the dominant one today, which would be cured by leaving Bath, England, and going on another trip. At least she would be paying for it this time – the advance on her book had just come through. Unbelievable, really, that someone was interested in publishing a book which argued that Darwin was, though not totally wrong, greatly misguided, and that we were all in fact descended from aquatic mammals, not apes. *Homo aquaticus*. He had to remember not to say descended from fish, which upset her.

It was not that he was envious of her success – no one could accuse him of that. After all, he had published two scientific works on salinity and aquifers, and last time they had travelled – to take the waters at Vichy – those works had funded them. It was a quiet but definite pleasure, in fact, to have her succeed in getting the advance, the prospect of spending *her* money for once. And the Australian dollar, he had noted in the newspaper in his hand, was unbelievably weak against sterling.

No, he was definitely pleased for her, especially as his next work, on water tables, was not going as quickly as he would have liked. And after all, their interests coincided – she with her love of research into fish and her yen for spa waters, he with his more rational area of research.

And wasn't that the secret of a lasting marriage? A coincidence of interests (both intellectual and self)? Yes, he thought with satisfaction, as he looked at her, excited about this new trip, this new possible cure, he did still love her. She did of course go off the deep end a bit with her theories about water births and babies born with webbed toes. Not to mention the significance of the little scars behind his own ears.

Remnant gills, quite common, born like that. Non-functioning, of course – had been sliced off when he was a baby. He did not like to think how much sway these gills held in her love for him. He liked to think that her regard for him was based on more than the fact that she believed he was living proof of her theory. But at times it was hard.

She kissed and caressed these gills when they made love – which took place, without fail, in their rather large spa bath, sunk into the bathroom floor. She was, in short, a most watery woman.

He thought of relationships in terms of aquifers. Love lay below the water table, endless, or threatened by pollution, able to be drawn up to nourish the pair, the couple. Difficult to contact, for the single person, love. He was grateful to be in a couple, and could not imagine life otherwise now.

In a way, they were the same. She too thought in terms of water, oceans, fishy ancestors of humans, bereft of their true watery element, forever in search of it – drinking, swimming, bathing, creating whole towns centred on spa water, whole birthing wards to allow babies to be born into water, where they instinctively swim.

'Shall I run the spa bath, dear?' he asked hopefully, leaning against the doorway.

'We no longer know how much closer we are to fish than to apes since you have hogged the limelight,' was her reply.

However, he noted that her cassette tape was turning, and that this remark was not addressed to him, required no response.

Her book took the form of a series of speculations addressed to Darwin, which she read onto her voice-recorder each night, and it was Darwin to whom this remark had been addressed. He supposed she did not feel like a *spa*, which was as much their private word for making love as *doing a cattleya* was for M. Swann and Odette.

He stood a moment, listening to these imaginary conversations with Darwin (in which, of course, the author was given no right of reply) and was glad of this third person's company in the house. He knew that his wife was either a revolutionary genius or quite mad. At first he tried to follow the arguments, but then decided that it didn't matter; Magdala had no need for him to follow them, as it appeared Mr Darwin not only followed them but was floored by their brilliance. Giles' own role was just to love her, mad or not.

'Why did we lose our body hair?' she was at that moment asking Mr Darwin. She had placed his tome, open, on the armchair opposite her. 'Olympic swimmers shave off their body hair to save a second in a hundred metre swim. Did our more hairy ancestors lag behind, get picked off by sharks, and thus favour the selection of the hairless? The streamlined body, smoothly shaped by layers of subcutaneous fat (which make the chubby, buoyant baby the most likely to survive), the jawbone shaped like that of a frog. All add up to *homo aquaticus* spending at least six or seven hours a day in the sea. The first tool may have been to open shellfish; imagine that, Mr Darwin. Making fires of dried seaweed and driftwood along the shores ...'

'The point, dear, get to the point,' muttered Giles to himself.

'When she emerged from the water, after millions of years, she was very different – now hairless, streamlined, and above all – erect. This is my explanation of the missing link, that period of twenty million years between the earliest fossil *homo erectus* and their more apelike ancestors. The fossils would be in the water, Mr Darwin.'

'Better you than me, Mr Darwin ...'

'And then there is the diving reflex. This exists only in mammals and birds that dive underwater – whales, seals, penguins, ducks. It only happens if the face is submerged, not if a mask is worn. So pearl divers underwater, with the face exposed, trigger an immediate cutting down of the blood supply to most of the body, but leave a good supply to the brain and the heart.

'And seven per cent of people are born with webbing between the toes, especially between the second and third toes, but they do not like to talk about it …'

'They certainly don't,' Giles grumbled, and at this point, he left the room, glad he'd had his own webbing surgically removed as an infant.

In the kitchen, he was preparing two bowls of soy and lecithin flakes when she called out to him again. 'Giles? Be a dear and find somewhere to stay?'

'Where?'

'Australia.'

'What, now?'

'Yes. Use the internet if you're too lazy to ring up.'

He glanced over to the computer and sighed. He placed the bowls to one side, put a tea towel over them, and crossed the kitchen to the little alcove that served as his workstation. She did not use a computer for her work, preferring the tapes, coloured pens, and the entire sunroom, which was her territory alone. Ah, the curse of having a partner who finds it difficult to get out of her armchair, the curse of not having a laptop to pass to her. Arthritis was a terrible thing, he reminded himself as he flicked the switches, plugged in the modem.

He had always been drawn to invalid women. There had been Coral with the vaguely weak constitution, the chronic fatigue. Alice with one leg shorter than the other and her special shoes.

Now Magdala, whose first words to him, over a café table with mutual friends, had been, 'Could you please select a cake for me from the counter, my arthritis is killing me.'

She had never spoken so politely to him since. Yet why did he let her join this string of invalid women he ended up looking after?

'Come and look at this,' she ordered.

A mystery to him, his destiny, he thought as he patiently approached her, listened to the newspaper clipping she read out to him from *Spa Weekly*.

Hot on the heels of poisoned water in Sydney, comes another water scandal from Australia. Wombat, called The Medicine Chest of Melbourne, where people have always gone for rest from the fast-lane, for a reinvigorating or relaxing spa bath or massage, has been hit by the shocking news that the local spa water has been affected by the same giardia outbreak that has plagued the city's drinking water for the last few years. All persons who have recently had a spa where water may have been ingested are requested to seek medical advice immediately. Symptoms of possible giardia include stomach cramps, diarrhoea and fevers. Local officials are shocked by the news and doing all they can ...

'So the trip's off?'

Magdala scoffed. 'The holy water at Lourdes is well-known to be highly toxic.'

'So you still want to go?'

'And the water that helped me at Vichy was probably radio-active.'

She was no more disturbed by the news than were the local Wombat officials.

The colours and smooth transitions of the computer screen as he searched out flights and accommodation soothed him with its precise representations of an ordered, predictable, immutable world. He began to believe that perhaps this trip would be as fine as their other adventures.

To outsiders, it could appear that this marriage was based on the search for a cure for arthritis, but he knew the arthritis was almost incidental to the real search. The spa waters themselves were the point. She was obsessed with them, they inspired her latest work. They were further proof of her theory, the fascination of humankind with baths of all kinds, rather than with, for example, swinging through the treetops.

Which proved her point nicely.

Did she really have the key to the origin of the species? Could she really prove that Darwin was wrong? Sometimes she tried to explain it to him, but it was hard to follow and her words – she could talk for hours without stopping – drowned him. That was why he went so quickly to follow orders, without question. The woman could send him under with words, once she started. Send him right under.

Parts of her work had been published, including one article about remnant gills such as his own. Before he met her he had been embarrassed about these scars, but she said many people had them, as well as webbed fingers and toes, yet all these obvious pointers were hushed up because Darwin was the man with the answer.

Admittedly, her published articles omitted to spell out the conclusions she drew from her facts. One article had been on the similarity between shoals of fish and ravers at a dance party because of an organ called the *sacculus*, thought not to have any hearing function, sensitive to noises over ninety decibels and inherited from a fish-like ancestor. Fish use the *sacculus* to detect vibrations in the water, swarming and moving in unison, hearing each other, just as ravers dance and move in unison, not knowing they are part of a shoal, their ancient hearing organ activated by the music. This article eventually found its way into a poetry supplement. When the editor had rung to ask Magdala for more such *cool poetic pieces,* she had hung up on him, saying she would never send him anything again.

Wombat? Trust the *Spa News* to find out about this most unfashionable spa in the Antipodes, which had sent him off trawling through the fishing nets of the computer after her sudden need for information.

In Wombat, they had known for years that it was just a matter of time before the water became affected enough for the bacteria to be detected. Now the news was out, the town did not die, as one might have expected. You'd think it would have been as quiet as any town now, but Wombat the illusion lived on separately from Wombat the town with a water problem. In the brochures, in people's dreams. The tourists did not become a thing of the past, shrouded by the flattering soft-focus of nostalgia. The baker was still open on Saturday afternoons, the Lakeside Hotel did not lay off staff. The fish and chip shop, a gypsy caravan of yellow and red fairy lights, did not become, as it had once been, the major dining attraction, and the Greek restaurant did not fold its starched tablecloths. Its surly teenage heirs were still forced to wait on tables while they waited to inherit the family-fortune-making café. The unemployment lines did not grow and the massage B&Bs did not close.

The water problem was under control, said the council. They said this for weeks on end, and journalists, wreathed in complimentary valerian and chamomile fumes, did not press the point.

With leather gloves and German hedge-clippers, Agatha was hacking at the blackberry bushes. She felt them grabbing at her, conscious, malevolent. The blackberry bush has a way of bending over the ground, and taking root again at the end of the branch, forming another bush; this is how the brambles can cover neglected ground so quickly. She knew this, but suspected them, nevertheless, of having a mind, a battle plan.

Falstaff speaks of *reasons as plentiful as blackberries* and in *Troilus and Cressida* it is said Ulysses is *not worth a blackberry*. She realised now, surrounded by them, hating them, how great an insult this was. Blackberries must have been everywhere even in Shakespeare's time. But the snow killed them off over there and without it they were taking over southern Australia. Real trash from Europe, she hissed, as she slashed at them. As a child, she had liked to eat blackberries from the bush, but now the sight of them, fertile, full of seeds, repulsed her. She gave a particularly violent slash to an overarching bramble and it retaliated, found her cheek and drew blood. She swore out loud. She looked around to see if anybody was there to hear. Had a glimpse of how a stranger might see her. Obsessive, crazy maybe.

Alone.

How small had she made her world? How empty? Yet she didn't want to fill it with memories from the nightmare. She had blocked them out with her work at the post office, and now she would do the same with the garden.

More brambles lashed out at her, her skin was crisscrossed with the punishment the blackberries were inflicting on their destroyer.

Every night, she stood at the kitchen sink (the bathroom floor was too unstable), dabbing at the bleeding scratches with antiseptic, thinking of the brambles in *Sleeping Beauty*. She and Frank used to read the story to each other, a particular version where a king and queen cannot have a child, though they long for one. Like the king and queen, they had waited five years before

Daphne was born. Princess Rose is born at last, but the parents are warned she will prick her finger and die.

It is strange how a story can know more than the listener. About the listener. She could not bear to remember this story – now that her own beloved Princess Rose had also not died, something worse, in a way. More mysterious. And since then Agatha had lived in a sleeping world of life without her daughter. Preserving all her things, waiting for her to come back, to wake up, so Agatha too could wake up from her enchantment.

Even the smoke from the chimneys stood upright and solid in the air. And the fountain froze, not to ice but stillness, with never a drop of water falling.

This was the still place she had inhabited, ever since that time, especially in her dreams. In the sunlight, she could fight it like the blackberry brambles she fought each day. But now they were threatening to enmesh her more deeply into the fairy tale.

Accompanied by her husband, who carries her carpetbag of books, Magdala is on her way to Wombat. Magdala, who does not see what is before her eyes, whose head is lost in clouds of myth, of ancient water underground, of ancient fishy ancestors. Magdala, who believes she has the second sight of faeries. She has been to Vichy, she has been to Baden, and her address in all data banks is now Bath, England.

She is on her way now to the only spa in the Southern Hemisphere.

Agatha liked catalogues. She had never put a No Junk Mail sticker on her letterbox at the lime-green flat, and there wasn't one at *Agatha Springs* either, so catalogues kept arriving, pushed into the thorns around the box.

She saved them all and went through them at night in front of the combustion stove – the kitchen was the warmest room in the house. She sat there after tea, her body aching from hours of work each day in the garden, a drink in her hand. A week of clearing blackberries had not removed the thickest brambles or even touched the roots, and the house and grounds were still prisoners.

She found the colours of the catalogues, the possibilities of possessing exciting *free gifts*, soothing. She licked bonus gift stamps, scratched instant win gold cards, filled in her orders. The momentary illusion of buying all those cosmetics, bath oils, books, saucepans, was enough to soothe her.

She then threw all the orders into the fire because she couldn't afford them, and anyway, the house was hardly big enough for what she already owned.

It was the process that stilled her mind.

That Christmas, the next-door tenants in the lime-green flat had sprayed their windows with *Santa Snow*.

Daphne had been sulky all Christmas Eve, skulking around her room and playing one particular Nirvana dirge over and over, when she suddenly emerged, with her *asking for money* smile. But instead of nagging about the Docs again, she had just asked for two dollars for Santa Snow.

Frank had been so relieved she had snapped out of it that he told her to get five from the drawer in their bedroom. The parents then had a row about whether this was or was not rewarding her for sulking. These details were imprinted in Agatha's memory, and his she guessed, though he was not a man to speak much about his feelings.

Arguments, while *the incident* was happening with their daughter. And that was the last time they had ever seen her.

That's what the police called it. *The incident.*

They had not mentioned the Docs to the police.

The fights.

The tattoo.

Nor the two hundred dollars that was missing from the drawer in their bedroom.

For some time after the incident, Agatha could no longer read anything except catalogues. Then, gradually, she found she could read old-fashioned novels, formula novels, ones that could be relied upon not to contain graphic violence. She had a box of Agatha Christie novels inherited from her mother, who had devoured them. She had never unpacked this box before. Christie, after all, was what her mother read – but Agatha had been to university and did not read *escapism*. However, modern novels seemed too bloody, too full of pain. She did not need tales of abducted girls, torture, rape – no, especially not tales of abducted girls.

There was one abduction in Christie, but even that did not disturb her. The reader was with the girl the whole time, even when she wakes up with dyed blonde hair (hers was dark when she fell asleep) and there is no mystery as to her location.

Christie's people were simple, usually motivated by money or problems remote from her pain. And Miss Marple tidied everything up. There was no ambiguity, no possibility that crime would go unpunished. Agatha fantasised about Miss Marple investigating her daughter's case. Christie's favourite weapon was poison, curare or digitalis, and this botanical element overlapped with Agatha's own interest in the plant world.

She started wanting to discover what this curare was, what digitalis was. Then she began to study with delicate pleasure the symptoms and effects of various poisonous plants, having, in the back of her mind, the shadowy man who had taken away her daughter.

In her dreams now she murdered the man with the help of Miss Maple (for dream logic omitted the 'r' and made her into a plant), who also helped her discover her daughter, at various ages, long after the police had given up the case.

She would wake in the morning, her muscles tired, to the double call of the magpies' screeching. Here, she could no longer hear that other cry, the one that haunted her. The cry of the magpies drowned it out, and she loved them for it. She spread breadcrumbs and soaked crusts on the veranda for them. They were huge, these magpies, bigger than she had ever seen before, and breeding furiously, with hordes of grey baby ones to teach.

She woke happy here, no longer hearing the other cry. The fire would still be glowing in the mornings and she would put on a shawl, stoke it up and wait for the kettle to boil.

Frank would like the way the house backed onto the forest of gums and acacias, where bushwalkers like him tramped through the paths that wound through the old goldfields. She walked down there to collect kindling. The roof didn't leak, the floor had no borer – though the bathroom floor was a problem. The damp, woody smell permeated the house now.

A huge magpie tapped its solid beak at the windowpane inches from where she was sitting. When she looked up it put its head to one side, knowing it had her attention. She grabbed a handful of breakfast cereal and went outside onto the back veranda. It was waiting for her, unafraid. Immediately two others birds arrived, warlike beaks and claws, carolling.

Now the jungle of brambles had been partly cleared, the line of yew trees disappearing away to the odd green circle around the old pump was visible. A pump shaped like a dragon.

This must have been the original Agatha Springs.

She sniffed the air. From the veranda, the smell from the bathroom was overwhelming. She would have to do something about it, but the blackberries possessed her for now, their tangled claws still gripping the land around the house. Their persistent fertility in the face of Agatha's hatred infuriated her. They scratched any inch of skin uncovered as if she were their personal enemy.

The scratch of a blackberry thorn was a particular pain. An ache. And when they clung to her, to the edge of her skirt or shirt, it was like a demanding child pulling at her.

She remembered now being annoyed with her daughter in the supermarket as she pulled at her shirt demanding some product displayed deliberately at her eye level. This memory wedged its way into her memories of lost Eden. It brought with it other memories – the fight, the missing money, the anger she had felt at her daughter before the disappearance.

And because the blackberries evoked these memories she despised them even more and decided to poison them.

There were, she discovered, two gardening shops in town. In the first one was Leif, a plump man dressed in walking gear that looked simple but was expensive. He looked at her in horror.

'You want to kill the blackberries?'

'They take over everything, all the natives ...'

'Just scrub, native grasses. Just clip the berries into a nice hedge, it goes well with the pines and the daffodils. Haven't you been to England? God it's beautiful, all those hedgerows and ...'

She began to wish she'd gone straight to the supermarket, where she would have been free to buy what she liked, even Kill-All, no questions asked.

Agatha couldn't believe it.

First, a shopkeeper who didn't want to sell her something. Second, a supposed nurseryman who stood up for that colonial invader, the blackberry. It was taking over the creek-beds, swallowing up not only her house but the entire country as far as she could see.

He lived, she guessed, in town in one of the neat streets of miners' cottages. Daffs, roses and dahlias all around, not a blackberry in sight, box hedges clipped to within an inch of their lives.

He did not understand her battle.

Suddenly there was a voice from behind her.

'Dirty eucalypts, dropping their bark everywhere, eh Leif?'

She turned and saw a wide-faced Aboriginal woman smiling sarcastically at them.

'Is that what you prefer? Bloody Aussie scrub?' the woman persisted, addressing Agatha now. 'Don't like that white trash blackberry, eh?'

Leif raised his eyes to the heavens. 'This is Eden, don't mind her. She runs the native flora shop down the road.' He lowered his voice. 'It's all politics to her.'

Eden challenged him. 'My shop's not all natives. It's got introduced species which thrive here, but don't strangle the local flora.'

Leif folded his arms. 'I told you before, gardening and politics don't mix, Eden.'

But Agatha was fascinated. 'I'll come and see your shop,' she said to Eden. 'I'm having trouble with blackberries –'

'Bloody blackberries? Whitefella rubbish. All the crap from Europe is taking over the country.' She darted a look at Leif, who scowled at her. 'I'll show you how to deal with that white trash. Yeah, just over the crossroads there. Can't miss it, *The Garden of Eden*, I call it. Great name eh?' she winked.

Then she was gone as suddenly as she had appeared.

In *The Garden of Eden* (which Agatha found to be disappointingly earthly), Eden herself was behind the counter, and a tall thin man in overalls (labelled *Kurt)* was arranging tubes of eucalypts on special at the door. Inside, callistemons, wattles, and native grasses were on display. Pink correas, ericas, and all kinds of bush tucker seeds. But there were introduced plants too, European and South African. There was even an Asian influence in the Zen gardens and Buddhas set among native grasses.

Agatha walked towards the counter. Eden saw her surprise.

'Don't get me wrong. I'm a reconciliation person, that's what. And I practise what I preach. In my garden, natives flourish, and introduced species have to know how to survive on our soil, in our sun – native conditions, get it – without smothering natives. Blackberry,' she spat the word, 'I hate the bastard.'

'You'll scare her away, Eden,' laughed Kurt.

But Agatha knew she had come to the right nursery. 'I need something for blackberries,' she explained.

He nodded. His eyes were green, and she moved her gaze from their intensity to the cleft in his collar bone, that lovely soft-skinned V. Big enough for her thumb, if she dared, and she lapsed into fantasy while he was advising her to rip out the blackberries by hand. Chainsaw them back, then dig out the roots. The only way to get rid of this European menace, to release the native beauty engulfed by it.

But she felt weak at the thought of more work.

'Eden said she had something ...' she managed to say.

He looked over at Eden, who was behind them, extracting from under the counter an unlabelled plastic sprayer, full of a pale gold liquid.

'Just don't use too much. And come back if you need any more.'

Agatha did not ask what it was, and she was not told. She paid for it and was just getting into her car when Kurt appeared, slightly out of breath. He offered her a potted callistemon, its red bottlebrush flower just beginning.

'A present,' he said, lowering his eyes, proffering it with both hands, as if it were a holy object. She took it. His fingers were long, strangely soft for a nurseryman, his arms ...

Sleep then and I will wind you in my arms
Fairies begone and be all ways away,
So doth the woodbine, the sweet honeysuckle
gently entwist ...

'Careful you don't use that spray on anything else,' he warned.

Ferociously she sprayed the poison on the blackberries, one of Christie's women determined to take up the responsibility of murder, glad she was using the strongest spray available. She felt wicked. But the blackberries must die. They were not co-operating with her environmentally friendly attempts to subdue them, and they would be punished.

And overnight, the blackberries disappeared.

By morning, all that remained of them was a black powder, which sank into the ground under the early morning dew.

There were no magpies that morning to wake Agatha, to drown out that other cry.

'Muu...uuum...'

Her daughter's cry at age three, laughing, calling her to look at something she was proud of.

At age ten, impatient.

The age varied, the pitch did not. Sometimes she heard it in the pitch of a certain kettle whistling, the pitch of a sax in jazz, the pitch of a train, and most often, in a crowded shopping mall where it somehow rose above the crowd sounds of other people's children. Sometimes she turned to the call, and it was another child calling her mother. Once she turned to see that three other women had also turned, only to see that child was calling to yet a fifth woman.

'Muu … uuum.'

They say each mother in the birth ward can recognise her own child crying.

What happens, though, when every child crying sounds like your own?

In Daphne's room, she sometimes sat looking out the stained glass-window, up to the pump and the green circle. She had uncovered a rusty potbelly hidden by false cupboard doors. It was still connected and she got it going.

Now that the blackberries were cleared, she could see that there had once been circular garden-beds up the hill, radiating out from the old pump shaped like a dragon. Had there been any rosemary, sweet eglantine, lavender and heart's-ease? The same ones she intended to plant again, her Shakespeare's Garden?

But before she planted, she would have to wait for the poison spray to dilute, the toxins to clear, wait to see which seeds might come up of their own accord, self-seeding now that the mantle of blackberry had been thrown off.

Here's flowers for you!
Hot lavender, mints, savory, marjoram:
The marigold, that goes to bed with the sun,
And with him rises weeping.

And so she waited.

In two broken pots flanking the front doorway, two twigs she had thought to be dead plants were the first to suddenly sprout green, shooting up, it seemed, overnight. Evergreen shrubs, which gave off an unpleasant odour if she brushed up against them in passing through the door.

Elsewhere in this earth, over the next few weeks, there grew other plants she did not recognise.

In the lime-green flat, sometimes Agatha would catch Frank standing at the door of Daphne's old room, unseeing.

He began insisting that they move to another unit, so they started arguing again. They threw words at each other, blaming each other for what could not really have been the other's fault. They argued, predictably, about Santa Snow. About the missing two hundred dollars. And fault. Fault.

They argued about car parking. Her obsession, as he called it. One night a Saab was parked in her spot and she had to join the cruisers looking for a park. She told him she was going to paint a sign in the kerb: *Please leave for No. 90.*

Or ruder signs.

He told her she was neurotic.

There was a dense fog on the morning that Magdala and Giles arrived at the airport in Melbourne. The plane had to circle the city for hours. Magdala meditated, then worked on her book. Giles did the crossword and then studied his text on the aquifers of central Australia.

Meanwhile, a hundred kilometres away in Wombat, you couldn't see a metre in front of your nose. The Sunday Market by the disused railway was hidden in white cloud. Mornings such as these were common in Wombat, but on Sundays a fog meant that the guest-houses, anxious to exceed client expectations and retain that market edge, sent out runners to see if the market stall-holders had turned up or not. To aid their guests' decision (shall we loll a little longer in the linen, darling?) of whether or not to face the delicious chill in the air, present in April just as it was in August when daffodils and violet grape hyacinths sprayed colour by the boggy roads, yellow and violet erupting in the cracks in the bitumen.

Ideally, a B&B is run by a giant Earth Mother who will serve surprises like stewed rhubarb and cook bacon and eggs, and you never have to do the dishes or make the bed. The bed will be four poster, preferably, and there will be a ewer and basin on the dressing table, which of course you won't use – your en suite will be either briskly functional (you will go out for spa baths) or will have a sunken spa with a view of the stars through a glass roof.

Magdala and Giles were looking forward to the B&B they had booked, wondering which type of en suite they would have. The details had been inadequate on the *Spa Holidays International* self-booking site, and they had not been able to get through on the phone number listed.

Agatha liked shopping at the supermarket in town. She liked the mechanised atmosphere, the illusion of order, the neatness, the little world where your every need could be fulfilled. But the supermarket and other outings to town were always threatened with dissolution. The voice could make the shelves of comforting goods dissolve like chalk drawings in the rain. Between her and the pain there was only this absence of the cry.

The front door was open when Agatha returned to *Agatha Springs* from shopping. Had she left it unlocked? She couldn't remember. They did that round here. She entered the house cautiously – the TV was there, nothing seemed at first to have been touched. But on the small table she had placed in Daphne's room, her private papers had been disarranged, put away in a different order. And the photos of her daughter and her husband had been removed from their frames. She looked around for them.

They were nowhere to be found.

She sat at the table a moment, invaded by her old fears, rising up now through her carefully organised net of activity. She sat there, not moving until she noticed she was shivering. The potbelly had gone out.

She realised, now that there had been an intruder, how totally alone she was. She could expect no visitors. Workmates from the post office no longer visited or rang even when Agatha and Frank had still been in the city. Ex-workmates had to be careful – after all, redundancy was in the air, and they knew it was catching. And there was the simple problem that it was suddenly hard work to talk to ex-colleagues.

You'll never guess what S did?

S?

Oh she came after you left. Anyway ... it doesn't matter.'

And contact with *Womanly You* was all by email. She realised she had never even seen her editor. She wanted Frank. She was so cold. She wanted his arms round her. He had not sent an email for a long time, and she was beginning to worry.

Spread out all over the lounge room of the lime-green flat, Frank had displayed the entire bushwalking range from his dream catalogue. The backpack, the boots, the sleeping bag, the water bottle, and dried food sachets. The water purifier, the Thermarest mattress, the one-man tent, and a mobile with email.

She wondered now if the regular emails were only to spare her from imagining that he too had been abducted, or whether he still cared about her. It was hard to tell from the words on the screen. He wrote that she had to move on, and he would return when she had admitted there was no point in keeping a place in their house for their daughter's possible return. She got out a map every time he emailed to see where he was on the Great Dividing Trail. Maps made her feel that all was explainable.

And at *Agatha Springs* she explored the maps and books that had come with the house. There were books about Eldorado, about gold prospecting, gems and metals. There were maps of bush tracks too and she told herself that soon she would venture out on some of the bush walks, starting with those outlined in red pencil. Those were the ones the previous owner had liked, perhaps. There was the blowhole where the goldminers had diverted a creek with dynamite to pan the bed. That wasn't far. And then a longer one called Golden Child Walk.

Supposedly because of a gold nugget weighing twenty-five kilograms and believed to be the largest in Australia. And in the shape of a small child ... however, this nugget had never been sighted.

Twenty-five kilos. How old was a child who weighed that much? Certainly more than an infant. She would have to get out the baby book and look it up. Once, she would have known.

A man was supposedly murdered in his sleep one night because he refused to divulge the whereabouts of the precious nugget. The so-called Golden Child Walk is a misnomer, as the nugget was not discovered there at all.

She waited another week.

Plenty of emails from her editor asking when the garden would be ready for Open Day, which she ignored, but still no news of Frank.

Then, finally, he emailed her that he was leaving the track, heading for the bush, where there were no marked trails, looking for Daphne's body.

It's a pattern. In the cases I've researched, they bury the bodies in shallow graves away from the tracks. I'll never find her any other way. You won't hear from me again until I find her.

She thought he had been walking away from Daphne.

All the time, he had been trying to walk towards her.

Agatha could not get the nightmare out of her mind. Frank, cold and alone, lost in the bush.

She called the police. It was hard to make them believe that he was not mad. Yes, he had headed into the bush along the Great Dividing Trail, alone, but then decided to leave the marked tracks.

Doesn't he know never to walk alone?

Never to leave the track?

He's not even experienced ...

No note to a ranger?

What if ...?

Why?

They checked the records and found that she had reported her daughter missing five years ago.

The *milkbar girl.*

'And now your husband's missing too?'

The policeman scratched his chin, exchanged glances with his partner.

Did they think she had murdered both of them? In a Christie novel she would be the poisoning mother – with curare, perhaps, or hemlock, and both their bodies would be dug up in the back yard. But in real life all she felt at the moment was humiliation at having the secret drawer of her emotional life turned over to strangers.

She showed them his last email and the ones before that.

Would they work harder now that they knew of the two disappearances or more slowly?

Would someone down at the station quote from Wilde that to lose one relative was a misfortune but to lose two was carelessness?

Or worse.

The police replied to her repeated calls saying that they would let her know if they found anything. But she wanted to do more than just wait for news of him.

If she was to set out to find Frank she would have to know a few tricks – what to put in a daypack, how much terrain could be covered in an hour, even how to read a compass. She wanted to learn that. So she rang the local bushwalking group, arranging to attend the local scout hall the next Thursday for the Introductory Lecture. After that she could apply for membership. That phrase made her nervous. She was finished with study, with exams – what if they didn't accept her?

She liked the idea of walking with a group of people for company, of always having a topic of conversation – the trees, the breeze, the wildflowers. Company without probing questions. They need not know she was learning in order to help find Frank.

Meanwhile, she studied ads for walking boots.

Italian-made waterproof trekking boots with Gore-Tex lining. $449.

Brown waterproof boots, midsole with steel shark, $269.

Signature boot for any activity from mountain hiking to touring, $249.

In the end, she bought brown Grosby boots, with *quality leather uppers, durable yet comfortable. $39.85.* From the supermarket. There were fewer tourists there mid-week, and the town was revealed without its gloss. She had a feeling that they all knew she was from the city. She felt well-off compared with those around her. Cherub-faced young blonde girls were pushing prams. Youths smoked cigarettes sitting in the gutter. The busiest days in the mall were pension days, family support days, dole days. The op-shops were full of girls excited over lurex tank-tops, boys pleased to find faded jeans, holes a fashion bonus, the fish shop crowded with takers for its all-you-can-eat-for-$6.00 (mid-week only – that is, no tourists).

Maurilia Meehan

Still no email from Frank, no news from the police.

There was an email from *Womanly You* saying that the sales department wasn't too keen on the Shakespeare idea, but that they would give it a go as a one-off. Could she ring to discuss. She could but she didn't. There was plenty else to do at home. She wore her boots every day and she got satisfaction out of moving her body, creating order, using her hands. She found these simple, repetitive tasks soothing. Hypnotic. Her mind, fixed on a present task, did not wander back to the past. Or to Frank. And that, after all, was her main game.

In an old house there is always work to do – washing old paintwork, cleaning dust, replacing nails. And then there was the endless fascination of the Fat Budget. She had thrown away all the old-fashioned books on calorie counting – fats were the baddies, not calories. She had a small calculator in the kitchen on which, more often than not, it was grams of fat rather than money that were calculated. In a way, they made a nice contrast. With money, the higher the budget the better. With fat, the lower the better. Avocado, of course, her addiction, on toast with butter slathered on. That must have been what was making her plump around the belly. She had started to wear looser clothes, no one had really noticed, but she felt fat. The more she weighed, the less she felt *herself*, so now it was fat-free yogurt, ice-cream, skim-milk powder, tofu in tamari, ginger and garlic. Well, it might be hard to continue with the tofu here. It would mean regular trips into town.

She started planting out a veggie and herb garden. Leafy greens, spring onions. Broccoli and beans she considered not worth bothering about – one crop and then it's gone. She liked solid all-year crops.

She laid newspaper and pea straw in thick layers over the old garden beds, planted lavender and aloe vera from the market in the circular gardens that now lay uncovered, radiating out from the dragon. Aloe vera she would mix up into a skin lotion, and it was also handy, she read, as a cure for arrow wounds.

And in the garden closest to the dragon, she started Shakespeare's flowers. Gillyflowers, columbines, love-in-idleness, cowslips.

And I serve the fairy queen
to dew her orbs upon the green.
The cowslips tall her pensioners be ...
I must go seek some dewdrops here.

She was confident that her editor would come around to her garden concept. Saw herself ready for the *Womanly You* tours quite soon.

She waited for the seedlings to develop.

And waited.

But the veggies she planted would not grow and neither would the simple cottage flowers. They gradually became covered in a black powder then seemed to melt back into the ground.

In their place, she watched unknown plants, self-seeded, begin to appear.

She must get out her books, try to identify them.

Meanwhile, she recorded everything she bought, how much it cost. She recorded what she ate every day, how many grams of fat. Of course the older books had claimed forty-five grams was OK – a typical meal of fish and chips exceeded this by five grams – but she always aimed to undercut this by at least twenty. In this way dark thoughts were kept at bay, the torchlight of the present aimed well away from the dark abyss. Now that Daphne's room was ready, now that she had contacted the police about Frank and begun to prepare herself to search for him, she felt she had done all she could.

And because of the magpies, the cry was chased away.

Still, a fear began to cross her mind that Frank and she were both mad. Their daughter had perhaps never existed, she was a case of *folie à deux* brought on by five years of trying and failing to get pregnant. There were phantom pregnancies weren't there, so perhaps there were also phantom children.

In her dreams, she and Daphne were hiding behind a shed in the backyard of her own childhood and she was sheltering her, arms around her, because a small bright thing she knew was a nuclear bomb was coming towards them. Just as it hits them, or just before, they both slip into a blissful state of non-being.

Each Mother's Day for the last five years Agatha had half-hoped for a call from Daphne. The commercials about special days for Mum, special presents, special bargains, were difficult for her. The street kids were given phone cards to call home. She saw that on TV. (Did they call home, or did they ring their dealers? Was Daphne a street kid? A dealer?)

Daphne had always made her a card for Mother's Day with glitter and love hearts, the style becoming more *recherché* each year. The last one had a bird's feather stuck on it with a little nest on a branch. She had it still, taped to her bedroom mirror.

But the year she had disappeared, Daphne had announced that Mother's Day was just a rip-off to make people buy things. There was no card that year.

On Mother's Day Agatha had always visited her own mother alone. The last time, Agatha's mother had opened the present she had brought to the over-heated suburban lounge room.

'Damn,' she said, and pitched it into the corner of the room. 'Fobbing me with off with damn chocolates now are you?'

Agatha's father, hearing her voice raised, came in from the next room. 'What's wrong?'

'Oh, nothing,' she said to him sweetly. 'I just couldn't get the paper off the present. Could you do it?'

And he picked it up from where it lay in the corner of the room.

'You know I never eat sweet things,' she lied to Agatha.

It was true Agatha used to try much harder to find special presents for her mother. But there had been more and more focus on the present itself as she had got older and now nothing satisfied, so her daughter had stopped trying to be original, inventive.

Books, for example, had to be vetted more and more. No modern thrillers with women chopped up in them or descriptions of dead bodies were allowed. The murders were to be off-stage or soft focus, but a murder there must be. No mad people, no children, no wars and the murder must be committed by *a nice class of person.*

This made finding a book almost impossible – and her mother had already read all the Christies. Anyway, as she had aged, had approached the ages of Miss Marple and Poirot, she decided they were most unrealistic portraits of old people. 'And a Frenchman would not make those grammatical mistakes, even if he's Belgian.' And she had even noted, in *Peril at End House*, some incorrect French.

So towards the end the only book in the universe, which she could read over and over again, was Iris Murdoch's last book, *Jackson's Dilemma*. About a man slipping into death who didn't know it, written by a woman slipping into death, who didn't know it. Read by a woman slipping into death who didn't know it.

Boxes within boxes, stories within stories. It made Agatha nervous to think that she might herself be involved in a situation, clear to an outsider, which she did not understand; her motives clear to the outsider, but quite hidden from herself.

As soon as her father was out of the room her mother threw away the chocolates again, then announced that she regretted having had children.

'It's not worth the candle,' she had snarled.

They sat still a moment in the heat of the room. Her mother was looking at her with hatred in her eyes.

'Shall I go now?' said Agatha eventually.

But at that moment her father came in with a plate of homemade biscuits and tea. Then he put the TV on with the sound off and sat there staring at it. He did not touch his biscuits.

'He thinks I'm trying to poison him,' hissed her mother, indicating the plate.

On TV there were scenes of refugees, a woman crying. Her mother became competitively unhappy.

'I'm sadder than her,' she said. 'Look at her, crying to be separated from her children. But she might secretly be happy to get away from them – if they are anything like mine. She's better off than me with my lot. I should never have had any of you. I wasn't the sort of woman who should have had children.'

Agatha didn't respond, so she turned to her husband. 'She just sits there. Can't get a reaction out of her. What's wrong with her? She takes after you – a cold streak. Bad blood …'

Her husband continued to stare at the silent TV, images now of a man hitting a golf ball. Her husband picked up a biscuit, studied it carefully, turning it over.

'Trying to poison him. Take me away from this mausoleum, down to the park. I think I'll have an ice cream. It's a long time since I've had an ice-cream in the park,' she added, letting her voice quaver to demonstrate how unhappy she was. (In fact, the last ice cream had been the week before, the last time Agatha had visited.)

Before she left her father read out from the paper a list of top gardening writers of that year.

'Ah, you see,' said her mother, leaning forward with pleasure, '*your* name isn't there, is it?' With a smile that said, '*that'll put her back in her box.*'

There were thirteen children, scattered now all over the world. Agatha, the eleventh, was the only one to visit and the least favoured. She was the receptacle for her mother's bitter sense of neglect. When Agatha had become pregnant her mother had said with a malicious smile, 'Now you'll see what life's got in store for you. And don't ask me to mind it – I've done my time.'

By the next Mother's Day, Agatha's mother was dead. She died just before the christening.

At Daphne's christening, only the twelfth and thirteenth sisters came. They had come back for the funeral, and had stayed on for the christening, flying in from Vichy where they worked as spa attendants. The twelfth was thin, neat, perfectly made-up, highly successful, clad in a black cloak, with just a tremor of the hands to betray that she was an alcoholic. They did not fly in together as they disliked each other as intensely as only sisters can.

The thirteenth sister was late, and the twelfth started drinking the celebratory sherry enthusiastically saying she was worried about the thirteenth. Everyone knew she was probably praying for the plane to crash.

Suddenly she asked if she might read the baby's hand.

There was a moment of surprise, then Agatha thought that would be fun and they gently opened the curled fingers.

'Would she have any lines yet?'

'Oh yes, the main lines are at their clearest. The others just come from experience, but these ...' she showed Agatha and Frank, 'the three folds of pink skin, these contain her fate.'

The twelfth hunched over their treasure like a black crow over fresh prey.

Frank turned away at that point, huffing sceptically, as the twelfth announced, 'Well, she'll have a charmed childhood, enchanted even ... and then she will have an accident with a sharp object ...'

Agatha's face paled.

Frank turned back to the twelfth. He had never liked her. 'You may as well say that she will prick her finger on a spinning wheel –'

'Or a syringe ...' muttered Agatha.

'You're quite off your rocker.'

The twelfth looked up at him, confused, as if truly coming out of a trance. It seemed to Agatha that her sister really had second sight, at least at that moment.

There was silence in the room as she and Frank stared each other out over the cradle. The baby started whimpering and he picked her up.

'Now look what you've done,' he said with satisfaction.

The doorbell rang. Agatha opened it.

The thirteenth sister swept in, dressed in a white fake fur cape, which she did not remove. Everyone greeted her, except the twelfth, but she saw the mood was subdued. The baby was still crying.

'She's just read the baby's hand,' explained Agatha, taking the child from Frank, rocking her.

The thirteenth frowned but instead of asking what had been predicted that had been so upsetting, she picked up the little hand, now a tense fist as the baby squirmed in Agatha's arms.

She looked into the hand. And her frown deepened. Agatha burst into tears.

'Yes, an accident – but not in a literal sense. Steiner, for example, says there is a dark force that can enter the soul, when there is a space between the child and the adult ... but I'm scaring you, I'm sorry. Don't worry, she will in fact only fall into a deep sleep ...'

'A coma?' spluttered Agatha, horrified.

The thirteenth took her hands. 'The important thing is she will wake up from it.'

Frank suggested tersely that both sisters leave. He opened the door for them.

Agatha hastily kissed the thirteenth before, with a swirl of her white cape, she was gone. The twelfth raised her sherry glass in a toast. Agatha grabbed the glass from the drunken woman.

'I think the christening's over,' she said, wiping her eyes.

Agatha's father was not at the christening, because the day after his wife's funeral he had taken himself off to a monastery which, apparently, had been expecting him. He had been planning it for years. He was allowed no visitors. He gave the house, everything, to the monks.

All that Agatha inherited was the cardboard box of Christie books. When she began to read Christie she began also to understand how her mother had seen the world. Agatha had expected murder to be central to the stories, of course, but was astonished to find that in the world of these books that her mother inhabited, *the will* was central – who was in it, who wasn't, who would inherit. In this world, people's primary motivation was to inherit, and they saw the elderly as blocking their way to riches. The elderly, as the Chinese say, held the purse of gold in front of them. Without it the young would tread them underfoot, laugh on their graves.

The other insight for Agatha was that murders were often committed using plants that grew in most gardens, like digitalis, or foxglove. She researched the poisonous nature of plants alongside her notes for the magazine article on *Daffodils for Beginners*.

Plant them pointy side up
leave dead leaves when finished
plant in clumps, not rows.

What exactly was curare, for example? *Strychnos toxifera, Central America, all parts fatal, but must be injected.* (Didn't Christie once use it in a drink?) When she looked up from her books out into the garden, strange, unwanted plants were thriving. Digitalis was in reach, just outside the window, and next to it was belladonna, which earned its name in Renaissance times when Italian women applied an extract of the plant to their eyes to dilate the pupils for wide-eyed beauty. Deadly poison. She now saw that these curiosities of the plant world were thriving in her garden as if they had a will of their own. It excited her. She saw herself offering a deadly tea to a man in a balaclava, a man who took the tea from her and drank it. She knew this man was her child's abductor, and in her fantasy she felt enormous pleasure as he groaned and died in front of her.

She now noticed murder cases in the papers, especially by poison. There was a woman accused of murdering her husband with oleander. She boiled the roots in water and gave him oleander tea for three weeks. However, it was not enough to kill him. And Agatha remembered that part in *Under Milkwood*:

Here's your arsenic, dear. And your weed-killer biscuit.
I've throttled your parakeet. I've spat in the vases.
I've put cheese in the mouse-holes.
Here's your nice tea, dear.

The world was full of seething, murderous impulses, one where these impulses were registered as normal. Agatha too now knew this impulse.

With a shock she caught herself. Would she end up in hate-filled pain, regretting motherhood, like her own mother? But the enormous gulf between her mother and herself was that, as a Catholic, her mother had felt she had no choice in the matter of thirteen children coming along. It was blow after blow, tragedy after tragedy, as her delicate hands became rough and worn with scrubbing and washing nappies. Now that women could choose, did her mother hate them for escaping without her?

Her daughter could choose and she must have bitterly resented not being bound to her by women's shared fate, the chains of involuntary motherhood. No wonder a murder story was her fantasy of choice.

Agatha felt the baby in her arms, the light warmth. She felt the two-year-old, heavy, with downy hair that caught the light. She felt the five-year-old with cold cheeks from playing outside. She felt the smallest possible kiss on the cheek the ten-year-old could allow outside the school in front of friends.

These times existed, occupying the same point in time, still happening.

She felt these in her body, unexpectedly, rather than actually remembering them.

That was how she could go on living.

Agatha's walking boots wore in quickly. She had good strong feet, long and narrow with high arches and strong ankles. Daphne had inherited these feet and her own earlier love for dancing. (Daphne had gone through a pair of tap-shoes every year.) Not that Agatha danced any more.

There had been no more news from the police, only questions. *Would you say the marriage was in trouble?*

Could he have just met someone else, run away?

And no more emails from Frank. Worse, her own bounced back.

In the scout hall, sitting on wooden pews ranged around the walls, were half a dozen bushwalking club members. She took her seat. There was only one man and he was leaning heavily on a walking stick. She realised that she had surrendered to the woman's world of clubs where women were unfailingly surprised to find, yet again, no men. The answer, she knew, was sociological – men in their forties moved down the age spectrum in their quest, and could find a thirty-something or younger. They did not even *see* women their own age. Unless, like Agatha and Frank, they had met earlier and the man still remembered the woman's best years.

The woman who was the tutor stood at a table on which there was a purple daypack filled to bursting. The tutor did the usual introduction routines and then announced that she would be showing them all the things they needed to carry. She opened her own supply and pulled out a battered white cotton hat.

'Bushwalkers are famous for their humorous hats,' she said tersely.

There was a slight stir then as a second man entered the hall. It was Kurt. Agatha thought guiltily of the callistemon, which had died along with most of the other plants.

The sun was very low and his yellow hair, spiky and beginning to thin, caught the sunlight, and seemed like a radiant halo around his thin face.

Agatha blinked away this optical illusion. He wore a white shirt unbuttoned at his neck, which was level with her eyes as he sat down next to her. That triangular, slightly damp indentation which men protect with the knot of a tie. That vulnerable place.

Agatha experienced that electrical circuit that bypasses the neo-cortex, scoffs at it in fact. There were pheromones, it was scientifically proven. Proven also that the liquid in every cell in the body had its own ebb and flow tide according to the movements of the moon.

Each cell contained a sea.

Each body contained how many of these seas? If a water diviner can sense water, dark, inert, cold under the ground, she was not going to doubt that this man and she passed electric waves between them. As soon as he sat down, she wanted to reach out, take his smooth, long fingers.

The woman to her right jolted her, passed her a whistle and a compass. She stared at them as if they had fallen from the moon.

'Pass them along,' instructed the woman.

So she passed them to Kurt, avoiding his eyes. It was like show and tell at school. What would be passed around next? There followed a first-aid kit, salt for leeches, moleskins for blisters (avoided by wearing two pairs of socks), sunscreen, a tent peg (for digging) and a scrap of toilet paper, another whistle, a two inch square of plastic which was a raincoat, and a litre bottle of water. Last was a squashed muesli bar in a no-name wrapper.

'Emergency rations. Not to be eaten except in emergencies,' the teacher said sternly.

'No fear about that,' Kurt whispered to Agatha.

They broke for coffee and more no-name biscuits, during which there was great talk of boots – runners-vs-leather, Italian-vs-Hi-Tek.

How old are your boots?
Where did you get them?

The boot, she learnt, was the opening conversational gambit for a bushwalker. She recognised brand-names, knew the prices of the others' boots and tucked her own cheap ones under her chair, while she chatted with Kurt about backpack brands, bushwalking shops (two in the town, as well as Disposals) while fantasising about placing her thumb in the depression at his throat, admiring his finely chiselled face, his slight Nordic accent (which she would find out later that he hated).

'Do you live alone?'

She nodded.

'So do I. It's great, no one to answer to. My son was with me for a while, then he finished school.'

They talked about the absolute *fineness* of living alone. He told her how he cooked every month, one Saturday. He cooked three different casseroles – curry was his favourite – and put them in different single-serve containers in the fridge. Each night he came home and opened one.

'And the great thing is, I never know what I'm going to have for tea!'

They laughed. Yes, she lied, it was great living alone. He talked more about himself, and she was glad. As he continued about the joys of living alone, she wondered if, like her, he was speaking falsely. She wondered if, like her, he had someone he would like to share his life with.

Frank would return. And then she caught herself thinking that she could live with Kurt instead. Marry him. She had not even realised she was in the market, as they say, for a lover until he had walked into her life. How greedy, how presumptuous. How needy, in fact, she realised she was. She was falling in love with the first comer. His voice, tipped by his lilting accent, nuzzled at her.

He saw her eyes were on his open-necked shirt, or his neck perhaps. Should he have worn a tie?

'Can I run you home?'

With that request even a golden-haired man assumed too much. She knew that by letting him in she would let him into her private nightmare. Then he would ask questions, shine a torch once more down into the black shaft of the past. Anyway, as she said, she had her own car outside.

'A coffee then?'

She hesitated.

'Pick you up after work tomorrow then?'

The tutor was turning off the lights of the hall. Agatha stood at the window, making sure that his car had driven off.

Why had she let him arrange that?

What about Frank?

She decided that she would not be there when he called for her. She would take off, just like Frank – at least for a day or so. It would be practise for her big trip, searching for him.

She was studying the map of Golden Child Walk. Flat ground along a creek bed, steep slopes on each side. The land was riddled with mineshafts, marked with two crossed pick axes. There was also a cross, marked by hand, in the middle of the creek. On the back of the map, there was a page pasted from a storybook.

Once upon a time, there was a miser who melted down all his gold watches, chains and plates into one massive block of gold. He buried this huge block in his garden.

Every day he would walk over the bare dirt, then the grass, then the bushes that soon covered it, knowing it was there, feeling secure, safe, loved by it.

He felt rich even though he lived in a single-room hut with a dirt floor and ate only potatoes he grew himself and drank only water from his own tank.

One day he felt an impulse to inspect the love of his life, his gold. He got a shovel to dig it up. His shovel soon hit something hard and he cried out in anticipation. He got down on his hands and knees and scraped the dirt away, tearing his fingernails. Soon the dirt was cleared. But what was this?

He cried out in despair. Someone had taken his gold and replaced it with a huge block of useless bluestone, heavy and valueless.

He tore the rock from the ground, his nails by now ripped from his fingers, his hands bloodied. The stone lay exposed to the sun but refused to glint or gleam.

He was poor. All he had was a shack and a potato patch.

Then he tried to work out how long he had been 'poor' in this way.

When had his wealth been stolen?

Why hadn't he suddenly felt poor at the precise moment it was taken from him?

If he had never dug it up, he need never have discovered his poverty. He would still feel happy, rich.

If only he had not dug it up he could have died a happy man.

She refolded the map, the story.

The walk was about half an hour's drive, and the roads were steep. Dangerous. But if she went away for a while Kurt would forget about her. Let the past stay buried.

Army Disposals. Tent, gas stove, water bottles. Then the supermarket. A dozen packets of instant noodles (calorie count two hundred per packet), skim milk powder, cereal, sultanas and teabags. Sunscreen and insect repellent. She spread the supplies around her on the floor of the lounge room. She wouldn't be here when Kurt arrived. He would give up, leave off his gentle, insistent attention. Perhaps there would be another email from Frank when she returned. She would reply, but she wouldn't mention Kurt.

She was running away from him, giving him a few days of unanswered doorbells to discourage him. She too would walk alone.

She braked suddenly just before a curve. What a horror it must have been to come along these roads with a packhorse or with a bullock cart, wheels collapsing around sharp corners, the whole cart skidding down that hill. She shuddered, braked carefully before the next turn. Drove even more carefully through the steep spurs of the high country, dreading encounters with truckers, their bullbars adorned with stickers.

I shoot and I vote.

Shoot a greenie a day, keep the doctor away.

She set off walking from the car park.

Frank was walking in country like this, his mountain pack higher, his body leaner than hers.

Alone now among the eucalypts, Agatha was surprised to realise that she actually detested the Australian bush and had never understood the songs she had been taught.

I love a sunburnt country

A land of sweeping plains

of rugged mountain ranges …

The bushwalking group, she now realised, would be a comfort with its mindless prattle. The opposite of nature-loving hippies, bushwalkers in fact ward off nature. Insecticides, repellents, sunscreen, sunhats, band-aids, moleskins, and always boots, and then better boots. The dream of a pair of boots that would – what? Comfort, protect, be aesthetically pleasing, steadfast, resilient, quick to recover, and always just yours. A marriage? A friend?

She was relaxing into the walk now. She smiled down at her own boots, nicely double-creased across the toes – they were only hers now, were broken in. A pet? A horse is broken in, after all. What did explain this warm relationship a walker has with her boots? You are not alone. You have your boots and they love your feet. Maybe other people felt like that about their cars. Cosy, encased, loved, protected. She had instead her tent which, it was claimed, she could erect in twenty-five seconds. It took her a minute in the house, not too bad, and she didn't have to step inside it. That claustrophobic feeling, fiddling under a half collapsed canvas that she remembered from her geography excursions.

Frank would be surprised to see her like this, out in the wild. She could brag about it to him in the next email. For she could not believe there would not be a next one. And that suggestion of the policeman's that he may have gone off with another woman. Impossible. They were fond of each other. It was just that they couldn't spend time together without being reminded. Those weeks. Months. Finally, years of waiting.

And Kurt? Before he came into her life her desire had been only for fantastic collages of gilded men rising from the sea, wearing golden masks and armbands, inhabitants of her dreams. Running her dream fingers along skin soft as her own.

In the abandoned gold diggings of Golden Child Walk, there was the silence of absence. The diggings were at the bottom of a steep gully, from which the bushy sides rose steeply. Through it ran a creek, once contaminated by the diggings, the pumps, the gold washing, the quartz crushing. She walked along the winding path following the creek and after a few hours arrived at a flat-topped grassy knoll to the left of the track. The grass was greener than the surrounding vegetation, and formed a circle about ten feet wide. Perfect for her first night of camping. There was even a stone fireplace, remnant of the chimney of a house. But then shouldn't the grass be somehow rectangularly green, the shadow of the old house? It was definitely a circle. She lit the fire with some twigs then unloaded her gear.

The tent actually worked – erecting itself almost as promised, in one minute. The sun was going down as she assembled all her equipment against nature. Her sleeping bag and doona. Her torch, her books.

She sat outside her tent, drinking the noodles from her Thermos. The air was chilly and the silence was oppressive. Yes, there were birds, there was the creek, but they were indifferent to her presence here. High on a grassy knoll, almost a perfect circle, she felt strangely exposed. Even inside her round tent she was sure someone was watching her. She lay in the sleeping bag, on the Thermarest. It wasn't as soft as they claimed. She could feel the cold, flat grassy surface under her bones as she drifted off to sleep.

The little voice calling out:

When the child was older, the call had a sense of indulgent tolerance to it.

Mu...uum...

Like that, it meant *really Mum, you are so silly*. That was the tone it had, always, at the time her daughter had disappeared.

Mu...uum, of course I've locked my bedroom window.

Mu...uum, of course I'll turn off the telly at ten.

Mu ... uum, you know I don't like those any more. I'm thirteen, you know ...

The very last sentence her daughter had spoken to her had been so ordinary. But she could never forget it.

Mu ... uum, everyone has Santa Spray. Mu ... umm, everyone goes barefoot to the shop. See you in a minute ...

In a minute. That minute. She had waited so long for it to end. And still waited.

Santa Spray, aerosol fake snow. It made her vomit. The sight of it. The industrial waste smell of it. Thirty degrees, and the collective Christmas consciousness in Australia wants snow. The word, the sight of snow, made her sick even now.

There was the cry again.

Before the indulgent stage. Its tone was simply claiming. Claiming. Claiming her steady still place, her mother. Calling out for water, to look at a shell, a leaf treasure. Again the call. Nearer. It seemed to be coming from just outside the tent.

The air was unnervingly still and thin here. As she lay in the tent she was sure there was whispering all around her. She re-fastened the tent zip firmly, shut her eyes to the shadows moving on the blue of the tent wall.

Frank would have told her she was imagining it all.

Kurt's red car was pulling up at *Agatha Springs* at the same time as Agatha had been walking along the creek track. He was earlier than the arranged time because he couldn't wait to see her. He loved her already, he loved the way her eyes had rested on his neck, his open-necked shirt.

She said she lived alone, and he knew she wanted him, and that did not happen often in his life. It was worth being early for. He waited, sitting in the car for the correct time. Expecting her to pull up in her car.

She hadn't yet.

He would keep waiting.

Agatha was too hot, then too cold to sleep. Each time she turned in the sleeping bag she imagined the earth shivered beneath her. She thought of the compass points, imagined the needle swinging wildly. The earth should be explainable in terms of lines and degrees. All should be predictable. But it unnerved her that true north was constantly shifting. In Victoria at that moment of celestial murmurings and shiftings it was actually thirteen degrees east of magnetic north. She shifted the angle of the compass so that the needle lined up with true north. Before her bushwalking classes she had assumed that someone armed with a compass, who kept walking, would go over seas, over continents, would arrive at the North Pole. It was logical. Now she knew that instead they would arrive at Hudson's Bay, Canada. And in a few years, somewhere else.

Better not to think about it too much; it made her feel slightly seasick to focus on this wobbling planet beneath her.

The red car was still there that night. All the house lights were out.

Kurt sat outside it in the dark with the radio tuned to *Love Requests and Dedications*. He knew he was in love because those same old love songs that had once sounded saccharine now tugged at his heart with their yearning. Agatha was a hardy perennial, he suspected, older than him, able to withstand the frost and drought of the emotions that had plagued him in relationships in the past – yet she still had the delicate appearance of the most ephemeral annual. This apparent contradiction fascinated him.

She lived alone, amazingly, but he would not pry into her past. He would wait until she wanted to talk about it.

There was a report on the car radio about that local legend, the werewolf. Another farmer had seen it.

'Came right at me …'

He wondered where Agatha was, hoped she would not be frightened by the appearance of the werewolf.

'Jumped on top of the car …'

Was it a certain type of person that the werewolf approached, he wondered? He hoped it would steer clear of Agatha, wherever she was. He saw himself protecting her from it.

People sometimes came to a new town to forget the past. He had made a fresh start here several years ago, was active in the local church, even read the lesson sometimes. And no one here knew about his record. He wanted to be, for Agatha, a fresh start.

He sat there, waiting for Agatha to return. Why had she agreed to see him if she was now hiding from him? He thought again of the way she had looked at him, like a cat assessing a meal. He'd heard about city women and one night stands. Perhaps she wouldn't love him after all. He caressed his neck where her eyes had devoured him and wondered.

Agatha was woken just before dawn by a noise outside the tent.

The world was a grey mist entering through the open tent zipper. (Why was the tent zipper open?) Agatha sat bolt upright, afraid for her life. A child, difficult to make out in the gloom, was sitting on her knees, her hands in her lap, watching her.

Just as Agatha was telling herself it was a dream, the child spoke.

'Are you here for the Golden Child too?'

'Wha...?'

'Everyone who camps in this circle is looking for the Golden Child.'

'I don't know what you're talking about.'

'Under the water in the creek.'

How long had the imp been there? Had she ferreted through her bags?

'Didn't anyone tell you it's rude to go into people's tents?'

The child considered this, her head on one side.

'They all think it'll make them rich as Midas.'

'What?'

'The Golden Child.'

But then, slipping out the unzipped tent door, the child faded away into the mist.

Agatha piled everything back into the car. Strange thoughts all night, tossing and turning. It was time to go home. She was ready to face up to Kurt. She missed her routine, was homesick already for her new house, her nest, after all.

She had allowed herself to be exiled from her own home. She drove faster than usual, cutting the corners she had edged around on her way up. She nearly ran into a logging truck coming up the narrow road but she braked and skirted the monster while he tooted her. She smiled to herself – the mountain had got into her already, or was it the effect of the thin air? The car was light to handle, responsive, a golden coach carrying her back to where she belonged.

She was surprised to see Kurt waiting for her, sitting in his red car with the radio on. He needed a shave, she noted, and wondered why he was looking so tired.

He said he was just driving by, hoping she was home. She mumbled an apology about missing their appointment the day before, and he helped her inside with her gear.

After her isolation in the bush she was pleased to see him and a little guilty about giving him the run-around. She made tea and toast for both of them while he was examining the old maps in the bookshelf, the faded books about gold. He pulled out one on El Dorado, the gilded man. She set the food on the table and they ate while he read out a text from the seventeenth century, his voice calm and peaceful, reminding her of her church-going days. Her rush of lust for him seemed to have passed, and as he read she determined that they would be just friends.

They stripped the man to the skin and anointed him with sticky earth on which they placed gold dust so that he was completely covered. They placed him on a raft heaped with gold and emeralds. For him to offer to his god. On the raft with him went the chieftains decked in pendants and earrings all of gold. As the raft left the shore the music began with trumpets, flutes and singing which shook the mountains and valleys, until the raft reached the centre of the lagoon. They raised a banner and signalled for silence.

The gilded man then made his offering, throwing out all the pile of gold into the middle of the lake ...

Agatha imagined all that gold, lying at the bottom of the lake. Had it been plundered? The lake drained? Or was it still there, unseen, making those who lived around the lake feel they were rich, living so close to the buried offering to the gods?

Kurt kept reading. She closed her eyes and saw the golden-dusted man walk towards her. High cheekbones glinting in the setting sun, the golden dust glittering. Naked. All of a sudden it was Kurt walking towards her, his eyes deep with desire. Shocked, she opened her eyes.

He stopped reading, put down the book and moved towards her. She leaned away from him. She didn't want him, did she? It seemed so long ago, all that. But he kissed her lightly on her eyes, her cheeks, her neck, and she discovered that yes, she did want him, and that yes, her thumb fitted as exactly as she had imagined into the hollow at his throat.

He was her gilded man, his face covered by a gold filigree mask, which she was reluctant to remove.

At ten o'clock in the morning, they were still asleep in bed.

A taxi pulled up outside and tooted.

Agatha got out of bed, pulled on her dressing gown and, quite grumpy from being pulled from her dream of a golden god (but then she looked at the bed and saw he was not a dream), opened the door. A man of about fifty was helping a woman out of the car, her black hair pinned up under a rather Edwardian hat with flowers waving in the wind – for there blew at that time a very cold wind from the east, a wind which had travelled up from Antarctica. She held on to her hat with one hand and in the other she extracted from the car a very large carpet bag – made to measure for her from French tapestry and the exact maximum size allowed for airport baggage. Suddenly the wind seemed to pitch her forward, so that she seemed to arrive on the front door-step without walking. (Who did she remind Agatha of?)

The man followed behind in the usual earthling manner, one foot in front of the other, and she was cursing his slowness by the time he arrived next to her. Whispering at him in a very married way, sending him back to unload three large suitcases from the boot. He was an unusually short man with a round face and large, pointed ears that stood out from his head. Agatha noticed two matching scars behind his ears.

The woman, who must have been twice his weight, stood straight with difficulty, as if to show that she could, then bent to sniff the strange-smelling, newly sprouted plants in the pots by the front door.

'Extraordinary,' she muttered, straightening up again. She turned to the right, seeming to be transfixed by the yew trees, towering up behind the house, freed of their shackles of blackberries.

'Remarkable ...'

The husband paid the taxi driver.

'Well, here we are,' the woman said, taking the stick the man offered her, tapping it on the doorstep as if to see if things were in fact solid down here in the Southern Hemisphere. Agatha was waiting for an explanation. The woman had small, peering blue eyes, and her hair was definitely dyed. She realised that it was Mary Poppins she reminded her of. Was she still dreaming?

'The Dewbanks? We booked ...'

'Over the internet,' added the husband.

Agatha looked puzzled.

'Good God, Giles, don't tell me you've screwed up again ...' And she waved her stick threateningly at him. He apologetically handed Agatha a folded computer printout.

She looked at it uncomprehendingly while the woman ranted. 'Ah, this place is the magical source I have been looking for, I can feel it! Just wait, Giles, I shall be well again ... and here I shall finish my grand work ... all shall be revealed to me here ...' And she took in a deep breath. 'The Antipodes, smell it, and yet we have a forest of oak, the antipodes, and yet we have the magic waters ...'

He ignored his wife, who was taking in noisy lungfuls of the southern air, and watched while Agatha searched the printout for meaning.

International Spa Bookings ...

Then Agatha saw it.

Agatha Springs, Smallest Hotel in the World.

It still existed, at least in cyberspace.

'We could be in Europe here,' said Giles.

'There are gums over there, see,' Agatha felt obliged to point out. 'But this isn't a hotel any more ...'

'Don't tell her that,' the man whispered to her. 'Please, she'll blame me. It's the waters she wants ...'

The taxi driver pulled off and Mr Dewbank looked wistfully after it.

'It's impossible.'

'Don't say that.' He lowered his voice. 'If it's a question of money, we'll pay double tariff ...'

'You can see this is just a shack ...'

She thought of her golden god in his bed, waiting for her. Why visitors this morning of all mornings? Would he be gone when she went inside, leaving behind only faery dust?

Giles was leaning towards her, whispering. 'Geomancy, you see ... the location ... she must stay here to get inspiration to complete her work.'

Mrs Dewbank didn't like all the whispering and hauled herself closer. She jabbed her stick at the paper in Agatha's hand. 'Our official booking ...'

'But there's been a mistake.'

'Look, this is Agatha Springs, the Smallest Hotel in the World, isn't it?'

'Well it was ... a long time ago ...'

Mr Dewbank's face was scarlet as he took Agatha by the elbow and pulled her out of earshot of Mrs Dewbank.

'Please, don't let her know I made a mistake.' He looked at his wife who was enchantedly addressing a yew tree. 'Just a few days till she gets it out of her system. Geomancy, you see ...'

'What?'

'A week? We'll pay high-season rates ...'

Rates? Money? She had to be practical – who knew when she would be ready for the Open Garden ... and there was only her column till then. But she only had Daphne's room, and that was sacred. Still, it had the view through the stained-glass windows, and the old iron bed. She could take out her papers, and the potbelly was warm enough.

She liked this little elf-like man, and she was curious about his wife's passion for the place.

'Welcome to *Agatha Springs*,' she smiled at Mrs Dewbank, picking up a suitcase. 'Come in.'

Inside, they were treated to the vision of a naked man sitting up in Agatha's bed.

But no one was in any position to be critical.

They loved the view. She made up the iron bed, gave them tea and crumpets and left them to sleep it off. In B&Bs she supposed guests were not permitted to hang around all day. So perhaps it would work out OK.

Kurt was waiting for her back in the bedroom. She explained what was going on.

'They say they can't believe I haven't exploited its potential …'

'Come and exploit *me*,' he said, holding out his arms to her. He kissed her, but she seemed distracted. 'Are you OK, Hock?'

So that would be her pet name. She smiled. He got out of bed and put more logs on the fire then invited her back to bed. They lay in each other's arms. They talked, they agreed. They agreed about curry (it was cleansing) and cats (lovely, but not for gardeners). She put her thumb, her mark, in the cleft on his neck.

'Why do you do that?'

She wanted to say that it was her favourite part of a man, but she edited her words. She was, after all, not new to the politics of love.

'It's my favourite part of *you*,' she said, and he laughed and kissed her and asked her if she was sure of that, putting her hand on another part of his body.

And it was true, at least while he was kissing her, that she was no longer sure of anything.

Of course, when you do fall in love, it always happens when you are looking the other way. It is always such a shock as, busy doing other things, busy putting it out of your mind, you realise you have been creating exactly the kind of favourable conditions for love to sneak up behind you, to hit you over the head.

By then it doesn't matter if, in the morning, she realises he has constant hay fever (why didn't she notice it before?) from his work with flowers. That he reaches for his nasal drops several times during the night. They sit up in bed, having tea and toast which he does offer to cook, as a man must these days, but which she cooks in the end because *she knows where things are.* Patterns are set.

And ever after, of course, those little blue and white nasal droppers would remind her of him whenever she saw one in the shops, though she would never have noticed them before.

'We don't know how many faery people are among us, and worse, they don't realise they are faery people themselves. They lose their second sight, their intuitions, their healing powers, through lack of practice ...'

'But the Bible says ...'

'Then there are those who died a violent death, who cannot let go of earthly life, and so are doomed to eternal return ...'

'Eternal life in God's garden, you mean ...'

The interlocutors were Mrs Magdala Dewbank and Kurt, who were sitting with Mr Dewbank and Agatha at the kitchen table, eating wild rice and mushrooms for the second night in a row. (Agatha didn't want them to feel the place was *too* perfect.)

'Of course, you know why this house is so damp, don't you?' Giles interrupted.

Agatha was glad of the distraction. It seemed Kurt was Born Again, and it had taken her by surprise.

'Yes, well it's the bathroom. Dreadful ...'

'Maybe not,' he beamed. 'After dinner, I'll show you something we found ...'

Mrs Dewbank had also had enough of the Bible teaching on the other side of the table. She turned to Agatha. 'You do realise, I suppose, what is happening with your garden?'

'It's such a disaster ...'

'All these plants that are coming up by themselves. There is a pattern in it …'

Mrs Dewbank went to continue, but Giles suddenly stood up and motioned to Agatha to follow him into the bathroom. The others crowded after them, and they all stood at the door while Giles pulled up several rotten floorboards with one hand.

Underneath, they saw a pool of water with a clear bubbling centre that made the green waterweed rise and fall slightly.

'It's mainly the waterweed that stinks so much …'

Mrs Dewbank pushed forward, her arthritis forgotten, and the two visitors started to grab at the waterweed, pulling it out like hair, placing it in the bath, while Agatha stood staring at the water, the rotten wood, the weeds in the bath, thinking of how very little now the house would be worth.

Had the agent known all along it was rotten? She'd have to do the stumps, the whole thing …

'Your own mineral spring, under the house. See that pipe there? That's why your water-pressure is so strong. It's piped into the plumbing.' He tasted it with a finger. 'We could hear it in the night from our room.'

(*Our* room?)

'It runs off under our bed, and down that old guttering there as it overflows. The dragon pump in the back of the garden must have drawn it up once too.'

She supposed she should be pleased, but she was too depressed at the thought of all this work to be done. Extra work before the garden was ready for its Open Day. She was suddenly grateful for the extra income the guests would bring.

'This is so splendid,' she heard Mrs Dewbank exclaiming, as if she had discovered buried treasure. 'Do you realise you have an actual spring in your own house?'

Giles now tasted the water. 'Interesting balance of minerals too … high in lithium, I'd say.'

'Splendid. A magic spring …'

'Why magic?'

'I told you, it's the geomancy of the place,' Mrs Dewbank said mysteriously.

'And the lithium,' added Giles, scooping up some more water in his hand. 'Let me fix it up for you, at least get rid of the smell. Fascinating project.'

He showed her the small crack in the eye of the century-old well. From it rose water that had been protected from light, kept deep in the earth's crust for thousands of years.

'The crack may mean it's contaminated,' said Giles. 'The clean water is mixing with the surface drainage water. I can fit it with a new pipe and fix the crack.'

Mrs Dewbank took a great interest in the unnaturally rapid growth of the self-seeding plants.

She and Agatha were standing at the strangely ordered rows of herbs and flowers that had established themselves in the gardens around the dragon.

'Here we have some dreadful poison weeds. That's hemlock, then we have belladonna, rhododendron taking over there behind the shed, oleander …'

'But there are some lovely cottage plants too – look, monkshood and foxglove.'

'Both splendid poisons. Actually, the presence of so many poisonous plants in traditional cottage gardens fascinates me – no doubt some were used medicinally, but the possibility of the good wife walking out among the privets and the berries and simply selecting a deadly brew for tea or leaves for a salad is, yes well, an intoxicating idea.

'The cottage garden, so romanticised, is actually a treasury of medicines and poisons, and there would have been be no autopsies or DNA testing to trap the perpetrator in those days. And then of course the abortificeants, very useful in those days … and those yew trees …'

'They seem to have doubled in height since I was gone.'

'Also splendidly poisonous.'

Agatha bent over some enormous, dark green leaves and stroked them. 'That's just rhubarb, isn't it?'

'Not just. The leaves, it's in the leaves.'

There was still no news of Frank.

Kurt came to see her most days. She was growing used to his company, though she did not encourage his obsession with the Bible. He was a close observer of people, and she liked his talk. He did not ask her much about herself, her past, and so she found him relaxing company.

They invited the Dewbanks on a walk with their club. Mr and Mrs Dewbank equipped themselves at the disposal store. The walk was just six kilometres, a hike down to a waterfall gleaming in the sun. The talk was as soothing as the grooming activities of monkeys. Set jokes about the leader being fearless, the whip being merciless. Everyone followed bush rules – stay together, wait at a fork in a track, and bitch about anyone who had to borrow anything from anyone else.

The leader, still with the purple daypack, liked to fill the air with her voice. She talked at first about the werewolf, but soon, like the others, about her car, her house, her dog, and her boots. She insisted bushwalking made her feel the same as when she was young.

'It's dreadful the ageing process, you know I feel like a young person trapped in an old person's body, I feel the same as when I was young, it's not fair …'

Why did this statement irritate Agatha so much? How could this woman feel the same? How could she be so stupid as to feel the world, see the world, as she did when she was young? Had she learnt nothing?

There was a fine art to achieving the right to walk alone. Or just with Kurt. She enjoyed matching her steps, her rhythm, to his. It was a matter of pace. Too fast and you caught up with the pair in front of you. Too slow and you lagged with the ones behind. In the middle there was a place where you could hear both conversations, without understanding either – a babble, like in a tram carriage.

Then there was a different pleasure when the walkers stopped for lunch. Sitting on fallen logs, with tender feet kicked free of their boots. The topics, again, were safe. Blisters. New boots. Cake. Weather.

Mr and Mrs Dewbank impressed everyone at the lunch stop with their ritual of gadgets. The air-pillow to sit on, brand new. They blew into it self-consciously, but no one commented. The mini-thermos for one drink of tea. The small wet towel to wash the face and hands after eating. The Swiss Army knives to cut fruit. All their equipment was eyed in silence, noted for possible later sourcing from camping shops.

There was the constant changing of walking partners because the tracks would often permit only two at once to walk abreast. It was like the barn dances she used to go to at school. Kurt was gone or yet to come, the annoying one would soon move on.

She preferred narrow tracks like the one they were on now, overgrown with a soft carpet of pink fallen gum leaves, to the wider access tracks, pitted with ruts from four-wheel-drives and wide enough for three or even four.

After her time in the bush, and knowing that Frank was out there, alone, she understood now why they talked all the time. The deeper into the bush they went, the more domestic the topics became. World trips, walks in other countries, (better, more impressive) and always the lousy dollar. Tales of pink wallpaper, patio areas, the bedroom ensuite extension, the second home. These walls and boundaries protected against the indifference of the gums, the strange animal droppings and burrows, the threat of rain, the bull-ants, the vulnerable body that at any moment could twist an ankle.

Huge red toadstools, wet fern trees and mossy trunks passed unnoticed if your eyes were always on the back of the person in front of you or on the immaculate, impressive performance of your clever boots (Agatha's less clever than most). If the chatter, the grooming talk was efficient, you could be anywhere. Cold, dark and indifferent the bush would be to any injured walker. She thought of Frank again. She shouldn't worry about him. After all, he was a high-tech walker with a mobile/email/phone and super boots. She wished now she could remember what kind of boots he had bought, and tried to see again his clothes, all laid out at home. But boots had been boots then, not best friends.

At the nursery, Agatha was watching Kurt fuss with the order of the punnets on display, arranging them by colour and size. Tall at the back, shorter in front, and all yellows and reds excluded, leaving her own favourites, mauve and blue and white.

It crossed her mind that he could be annoying, slightly obsessive, and this reassured her that she was not falling in love with him. He saw her and blew her a kiss, discreetly – they didn't want Eden to know, or it would be all over town. *He's too young for her, he couldn't be interested in her, she must be ten years older than him.* It was nice to think about kissing again. A non-Frank. So long since she had kissed a man, on the mouth, soft and lingering, wanting more.

At the counter, she asked for heart's-ease. While Kurt fetched it, Eden asked about the blackberries. Agatha was about to ask about the black powder, about the way the brambles had disappeared unnaturally quickly, when Kurt interrupted, holding the punnet of heart's-ease.

'For shady areas,' he advised her.

So she didn't ask Eden why nothing she planted grew, why only the self-seeded plants grew, arranging themselves as if the garden had a memory. She would try the heart's-ease anyway. She had to get this Shakespeare thing under way.

At the counter, she noticed a copy of *Womanly You.* It was open at The Happy Hock's column.

'A bit basic for you?' queried Agatha, testing.

'Yeah, but whatever she says in it, women come in and ask about. If she reminds them it's time for daffs, there's a rush on daffs. Or roses, or …'

Flattered, she couldn't help revealing who she was. Her other life.

'Wow …'

He beamed at her, asked her where Mary-Mary was hiding.

'She's around.'

She did not like that line of talk, so they talked about her garden. She told him about the Shakespeare project, which was why she wanted the heart's-ease.

'And any other cottage plants you have – lavender …'

She knew it probably wouldn't grow, but she had to keep trying.

'Cottage plants, this way, madam, roses …'

'No roses. I hate thorns.'

'Ah, but do you know what's just come in?' he said. 'I have a thornless hedge rose …'

'Absolutely no thorns?'

'Thought you'd like that. I'll deliver it tonight, if you like.'

She knew he knew she knew she could take the dry-rooted rose then and there. She had her car. But this subject, as lovers know, was not roses or cars.

She said yes.

That night in bed, while making sporadic love under cover of darkness, he started to ramble on about fertility, cross-pollination and the proof of The Universal Plan.

'How else would it know how to grow to be a tomato, a columbine and not another flower?'

He talked about self-seeded plants. 'My favourites, springing up everywhere out of love of life.'

(She thought of what her mother had said, how she had hated agapanthus for the same reason, had called her after it.) Agatha had not been to bed with a Born Again before but she was becoming adept at changing the topic whenever religion arose. Now she turned the conversation to talk about the local werewolf, roaming at night in the hills according to the headline in the local paper, the slogan of which was *All the news, if there is any.*

Kurt seemed to believe it existed.

'Bible people should not believe in werewolves, should they?'

He kissed her in reply, then changed the topic utterly.

'You don't want to talk about it, do you? I can tell. You know, running a nursery means I have to study people as well as plants. Next time you come in, I'll show you my theory of people.'

Eden was away. The two lovers sat together behind the counter, drinking coffee and observing the different customers rushing or dawdling along the outdoor aisles of plants, the indoor punnets of flowers.

'If only they knew the Happy Hock was watching them,' he murmured, holding her hand as he explained to her that there were eight distinct types of garden lovers, with eight distinct needs and ambitions. He believed this was part of being a nurseryman, to study these types, cater for them all.

'Over there', he whispered, 'is the Fashionable Gardener, my least favourite type.'

Agatha noted the tall thin woman in a red beret talking in a loud voice to her companion about a certain garden seat she was looking for, 'as featured in *Style*'.

'Full of bravado and less competent than they appear. Gardens full of half-done work. They prefer garden furniture and water features, and treat plants as props in their search for a look inspired by their gardening magazines.'

And so he shared with her, like a subversive voice-over, the way he amused himself each day. She listened, watched his hand on hers, feeling its heat, or observing the way he held a coffee mug with all fingers. Because he did it that way she liked it, thought it was a good way to hold a coffee mug, feeling the warmth in each finger. Surreptitiously, she adjusted the way she held her own mug, awkwardly, two fingers through the handle.

Agatha knew that she had to please her readers but she had never thought of there being so many types to please. His acute observation of human types surprised her – she had been prepared to learn about gardens and plants from him (in fact she needed to if her gardening 'career' was to continue) but not about people. She admired his finely observed comments, slightly sending himself up, the interest he took in the customers around him. She had assumed she wrote for beginners, and that there was only one type.

'Over there among the arches and the water features is the Demanding Gardener – the garden emerges as a testament to hard work, rather than to planning or overall vision. They love the garden as a means of keeping their hands busy, they like to build structures and tidiness is more important than aesthetics.'

'What about me?' she asked, as one inquired about star signs.

'Ah, the Creative Adventurer – gardening becomes a way to a richer life, an escape from a destiny they feel they have little control over ...'

But what happens when the garden is uncontrollable?

She looked away from him. Her coffee cup was empty.

'It must be time to go.'

'You will achieve what you set out to do ...'

This sounded more and more like a star chart, so she stood up.

'We'll see. Well, I haven't really been a gardener till now.'

'What? The Happy Hock not a gardener? What about your property in the city? A hundred years ago, you know, a gardener could never have owned his or her own garden. Now we can all have our own part of God's Eden.'

'Did I hear my name mentioned?' smiled Eden, suddenly approaching with a tiny African violet in purple paper for the woman in the beret.

'Coffee break, eh Kurt?' she said reprovingly, tying the paper with raffia.

'I'm just going,' said Agatha.

'Is he giving away our trade secrets? I taught him everything he knows. Look, there's an Instinctive Gardener – you recognise them quickly – they don't hover around the gardening books, but they love to talk gardening. They enjoy sweat and work almost in a trance in complex gardens of herbs, vegetables, natives and exotics.'

Eden walked away towards the Instinctive Gardener, who was calling her.

'Which type is Eden?'

'She would have to be The Deliberate Gardener. Very patient, they adopt causes and are very knowledgeable about the plant groups they prefer. Not to be confused with that Pragmatic Gardener over there among the power tools. No sentimentality, they love hedge clipping with power tools and they see a garden as a way of increasing the value of their home. Always sweeping up leaves, mowing and generally denuding the landscape. But Eden's a mix, she's got a lot of the Harmonious Gardener, who feels a strong sense of responsibility for the environment. They see their role as a custodian, letting plants grow naturally. But they are not dogmatic.'

'And what are you?'

'I'd have to be a Sentimental Gardener, the type who tries to grow blue poppies, for example, when it's simply not as cold here as in Tibet where they thrive. Gardening is our mission in life, and we become very attached to our special plants, like pets. We are successful at growing highly temperamental species and treat them as surrogate family members. We feel a loss when the plant dies. And,' he laughed, 'we are extremely attractive people.'

'Do you believe in all this?'

'Yes, but we're all a bit of a mix, aren't we? After all, I could say you were the Creative, but when I see you ripping out the blackberries, you look like a Pragmatic.'

'But you talk about it as if you are really serious about it.'

'Look,' he smiled, 'I'm just talking about it as a way to chat you up.'

She wondered if there was a category called The Direct Gardener.

That night, the town is shrouded in fog. People driving through it report that the werewolf bounds into their headlights, stares at them then leaps away again. Some say it is a kangaroo, others a feral cat, but those who see it swear otherwise.

And around Agatha Springs the ragged, inexorable, pharmaceutical garden is spreading like Marvell's monstrous vegetable love, *vaster than empires*.

Part Three

I am back again.

The front door is locked, so I go around the back, where there is a light on. I carefully edge the door open, shivering in my thin rags, the cold suddenly intensified by the rush of warm air from inside.

The pair of silver Doc Martens is on top of a packing case. I know now that I am in the right place. But there is a woman sitting on the bed, in what must be my room. She has shiny black hair, little peering blue eyes and looks just like Mary Poppins. The white witch with powers to come and go on the strength of the wind. There is even her enormous carpetbag by the wall ...

The two stared at each other. Mrs Dewbank, normally most effusive, did not rise to greet the new arrival. Instead, she looked her up and down.

'I knew you'd come,' Mrs Dewbank said quietly.

In a breathy voice, as if she had laryngitis, the girl tried to cry out. 'What are you doing in my room? Get out.'

She began hitting at the woman with her backpack, a ragged thing bejewelled with stickers.

The noise made Giles rush in from the garden.

'What's going on ... for heaven's sake ... who are ...'

But the girl broke off her attack when she saw him, and disappeared into the dusk outside.

'It's *her*,' said Mrs Dewbank to her husband, who nodded, pretending to understand.

Agatha was unpacking her shopping onto the kitchen table – the Dewbanks ate a lot of food. She did not hear the door open behind her.

'Hi Mum,' she heard a voice whisper.

She felt a shadow to her right. She turned to check that the voice was not, as usual, in her head. The voice that would complete her world.

The young girl with dyed black hair at first seemed tall, but this was just the effect of her platform boots. The soles were six inches thick. She took small careful steps in them, in danger of toppling off. In other decades, they would have been considered orthopaedic shoes, rectifying some unfortunate abnormality at birth. She was awkward as she came towards Agatha – she limped quite badly, as if her left foot was injured.

Agatha wanted to pick her up like an infant, rock her, swing her up and down. She reached out and hugged her, but the girl kept her body well away, surrendering only her arms and her cheek, for the kiss.

'Haven't you got any meat?'

'I'm a vego.'

While Daphne ate lentil soup and bread rolls, thickly buttered, Agatha peered into her face. Her skin was ashen and she was alarmingly thin. Her voice was almost inaudible. She didn't want to talk about the night of the disappearance.

She hung her head when Agatha tried to question her, speaking of dizziness and weakness.

'Later, Mum, I'll tell you later.'

She had arrived with just a backpack full of black velvet skirts, net T-shirts like spiders-webs, and torn shawls.

Her eyes seemed darker. Agatha tried not to stare at her, and stopped herself from hugging her too often. She didn't seem to like it. What had happened to her to make her shrink from human touch? The man ... the blue car ... Agatha knew she mustn't rush.

It had been five years ago, she was taller now and her naturally blonde hair was dyed black into a shock of matted fur. The hairstyle was common in town. What upset Agatha was that she was so thin, and seemed to have little strength.

She had not asked about Frank, and Agatha decided to wait until she did. After all, it would be difficult for the girl to learn that her father was missing.

It was the same with the police, when they heard the *milkbar girl* was back.

'Can you tell us anything about him?'

'I can't remember.'

They came around every day to talk to her until Agatha felt they were harassing her and so she started to tell that them Daphne was resting. She would talk to her mother first, she told them, that was normal. The police stood outside when they were talking to Agatha. Eventually, they said, they would have to go inside, rehash the night of the disappearance with her. Every painful detail. But they agreed that Daphne was not ready to talk yet. They gave Agatha a copy of the police report of the night. Of course she already had it. It said nothing really.

Dark night. Blue car ...

When she came inside, her daughter saw the paper in her hand.

'What's that?'

'The report of the night.'

The girl held out her hand, fingers trembling, and she took it away with her into the bedroom.

Agatha took this as a sign that she would come around to talking about it in her own time. Perhaps she would even give the police the information they needed to catch this man.

The man in the blue car.

Mr and Mrs Dewbank of course packed their bags to make room for Daphne. There was another B&B on the hill overlooking the house, where they went after dinner.

'Just act normally,' Magdala told Giles as they went towards the dinner table, for perhaps the last time.

At that last meal together (tofu in satay sauce, except for Daphne, who had rare lamb chops) Mrs Dewhurst dominated the conversation as usual, which suited everyone, as the girl did not want to talk. At the table, Daphne soon buried her head in the local paper, sucking her chop bones noisily. The headline was about the werewolf, sighted closer to town than ever before by a reliable witness.

Meanwhile, Mrs Dewbank's dining companions lost the thread as she raved about this town, this house, being central to her mythic research in which fish, definitely, were a theme.

'But are there any fish in underground water?' Agatha gamely asked her.

'An ancient salamander perhaps? What do *you* think, Giles? Hmmm?'

'I'll look it up for you, dear, interesting question.'

But he knew that if salamanders had fitted into her master plan, her theory of evolution, she would have found out for herself.

Of course when you have a Total Theory, as his wife had, everything slotted into it. She was explaining to Agatha, for example, about shopping.

'The selection of colours, fashions changing with the seasons as they do. Even the catalogues that fill this house, I notice. Just nostalgia for the seaweeds and bright corals in the ocean, from which some fish actually construct splendid homes.'

Gardening next, she was explaining away.

'The need to recreate the sea floor with its green, waving, delightful flora. Lawns especially revealed this atavistic desire – and of course swimming pools as a sign of real success in the world – that is self-evident.'

'More greens?' laughed Agatha, passing around the bowl, hoping there was not too much garlic. She had to buy her greens in town – the lettuce and garlic still refused to grow.

It crossed Agatha's mind now that whenever she passed around food, she could be poisoning everyone at the table. Quite easily. It gave a certain dignity to food preparation that she felt it had previously lacked. A car passed on the road outside, the stereo blasting out a techno *doof-doof*.

'And that noise ... a splendid example of a sonic wave, the same waves fish communicate by ...'

'The point, dear, the point ...'

Giles had heard it all before. Yes it all fitted, but sometimes he wondered if this meant, necessarily, that she was right.

After this last dinner with the Dewbanks, Daphne told Agatha that she didn't want them to visit again. 'It's not as if they're family,' she explained in her feathery voice.

But if she cared about family so much, Agatha wondered, why had she still not asked about her father?

Agatha dreamed that night that the werewolf had taken her daughter.

She had wandered too far from the track along the creek in the dark on the way to the milk bar, and the wolf-man grabbed her ankle, toyed with her awhile.

Ate her.

Daphne began to give Agatha snippets of information, but never enough. It was amnesia, they had said at the hospital.

'Which hospital?'

They had helped her find out where Agatha lived.

'But which hospital?'

She said she couldn't remember that. 'But not the local one,' she added.

Then she said she was dizzy and had to lie down.

She still had not asked about Frank.

Daphne did not seem to be recovering her strength. Agatha called a doctor, who diagnosed severe anaemia. He suggested she stay overnight in the hospital, and she agreed to, if Agatha stayed with her.

Her blood tests showed even less promising news. Her blood count was so low that the doctor thought she must be losing blood through the intestine. But every test was negative.

The doctor suggested a blood transfusion but the girl said she was afraid of needles. Agatha remembered the prediction of her sister at the christening, that the baby would be pricked by a sharp object, fall into a long coma.

Finally, the doctor talked her into an injection of iron. The girl screwed up her eyes, looked the other way while it happened. To Agatha she looked about three years old. Her toddler back home

110

again. On the way home, Agatha was elated that her daughter seemed to have more colour already. But the next day, she was as pale and weak as ever.

Agatha suggested they go back to the hospital. The girl frowned, impatient.

'No. I'm always like this. I just went so that you could see that there's nothing they can do for me. I won't see any more doctors. I'll never get better.'

'Don't say that.'

She took her iron tablets and Agatha cooked liver and meat, the middle still raw, just as Daphne had requested. It made Agatha nauseous to watch her eat it, watch her mopping up with bread the warm blood that oozed from the meat onto her plate.

The girl ate so much – how could she stay so thin? Agatha read all the magazine articles on bulimia and listened for the sound of induced vomiting in the bathroom, but could never catch her at anything like that.

Agatha woke in her bed to see an ashen figure towering over her.

She turned on the bedside light to examine her distraught girl. She was crying.

'Sit down, darling,' she said, taking her hand.

But the girl saw a stranger in her mother's bed and drew back. She had never met him before.

'Why is he here? I *hate* him.'

'But I told you he was coming ...'

'I don't want him here. I don't want any men here after ...'

Kurt sat up in bed, half asleep. 'I'm sorry,' he muttered, 'I'll go.'

'No, she's just ...'

But the girl glared at him with frightening venom.

'Get out of my mother's bed and leave us alone, why don't you?' she hissed.

The three of them were motionless in the light of that single lamp. Then a tremor seemed to seize the girl and in a staccato voice she said to Kurt, 'I hate what you look like, what you are and I hate your dumb foreign accent.'

Kurt was the first to move. He got out of bed, pulled on his clothes and went to kiss Agatha on the cheek. But she turned away from him.

'I'll call you,' she said to him as he left the room. Her daughter immediately crawled into the warmed space that he had left by her mother, a small triumphant smile playing around her lips.

It seemed that whenever Kurt visited, the girl's dizzy spells worsened. He agreed, reluctantly, to stop coming.

'Just till she settles down,' Agatha assured him.

But he had seen other households where adults lived in fear of upsetting teenagers and he did not like it. He started to park his car outside in the dark, waiting for Agatha to come outside. The girl noticed.

'It's disgusting, Mum. He's too young for you. You've got grey hairs … look. Anyway, he's always sneezing. And leaving these little things behind. What is it?'

She held out the blue and white nose dropper.

Agatha went to take it from her, but she pulled her hand away.

'I'm putting it straight in the bin,' said her daughter.

So Agatha and Kurt met at the nursery, and sometimes they went for a ride in his car up to Golden Child Walk, where they did what teenagers do.

But she did not feel like a teenager.

She remembered that even the first time with him, when they had sat by the bedroom fire, they had first touched each other, they had drunk wine, they had not noticed the sun go down, but it had not felt new for her. Each experience comes at you fresh when you are young – this is the first boy with hair exactly that colour that you have ever seen. He is overwhelmingly beautiful and so is the whole world. This is the first time you have kissed someone there, or there ... and this is the first time in the history of the whole universe that the shadows of the moon have fallen on you and on him, in that particular way.

And the first time since the dawn of creation that two people have made love on a white shag-pile in front of an open fire with the moonlight streaming in. Have cried like this, made up again like that. Now, like one negative imposed upon a previous dozen, each time and place and lover conjured up another one – that other shag-pile, that other moon, that other fire, that other red wine spilt, so that yes, the man with the hair like this is half like that one, but Frank was blonder, the moon felt like that in Venice, didn't it, or was it Amsterdam that night? And somehow her ownership of the event, the time, the person, slipped from her back to where it belonged, into the overarching sky, the endlessly repeating universe.

But it was not sad that it was illusion that this love belonged just to them. To her. To him. Because it passed through her. Through him. Through everything.

Always.

Agatha noticed the odd speck of blood in the toilet bowl. Her own periods had been barely existent for over a year. (She was relieved to be able to stop bothering with contraception.) She assumed it was Daphne's period, said nothing, just flushed it away. But it crossed her mind that the girl's periods must still be heavy, close together. She felt sorry for her, remembering how Daphne had always had a lot of trouble with menstruation. It had begun earlier than most of her friends, and they were so heavy that she often stayed home from school for three days a month. Bloodstained sheets and underwear had piled up in the laundry and she would often go without changing her pads until there was blood on the seat when she stood up. She was not embarrassed by this – Frank had been more embarrassed than she was.

In fact, she had seemed to be fascinated by the bright, fresh blood that her body had produced, even lying in the bath until the blood coloured the water pink.

Mrs Dewbank was standing at the window of the modern custom-built B&B overlooking *Agatha Springs*. She put down the binoculars through which she had been inspecting the place.

'Heaven and earth must part for the return of the prodigal daughter,' she muttered.

'That's a bit selfish, dear. I mean, Agatha didn't even want us there in the first place.'

'Nothing to do with that … and did you hear that creature call me Mary Poppins, under her breath?'

Giles smirked at this. 'Not the first image that would come to mind, dear. Let's give them a couple of days' rest before we visit again.'

'Visit? I wouldn't be surprised if we were turned away now that *she* has arrived.'

There was a knock at the door. Mr Dewbank answered it.

'Your wife's spa is ready.'

Mrs Dewbank had pointedly informed them that she wished to have a *single* spa.

'Hope you put in plenty of valerian,' he muttered.

Mrs Dewbank had found the spa satisfactory. Mr Dewbank had not. The valerian had had little effect.

'That house,' said his wife nodding at the window which gave onto it, 'has a dark past.'

'What's that, dear?' He was trying to enjoy his eggs and tomatoes.

'I told her that I knew what she was on about, ever since she came limping in that morning. She didn't fool me.'

He put down his knife and fork, wiped a little grease from his lips. 'What *is* she on about, dear?'

His wife only creased her brow and narrowed her lips. She loved being mysterious – no doubt it was something to do with fish, he supposed, and sighed.

'What's wrong with her foot, I wonder. Shame, such a pretty girl.'

'I can tell you what's wrong with her foot. In myth we have the Queen of Sheba who had the webbed foot of a goose.' She reached into her bag for a thick, worn book. 'Here's a print from Ulm in 1492 illustrating it. See her left foot? We also have the same image here in *The Faerie Queen*, see?'

She thrust the book between his eyes and his plate of food. He was not best pleased – the eggs were delicious, but getting cold. Eventually she withdrew the book and he recommenced eating, saying with a mouthful of luke-warm egg, 'The point, dear, get to the point.'

'Faeries,' she announced, 'can replace any child but …' She raised her finger and bounced it rhythmically as she recited.

'It's not in our power,
To incarnate ourselves …
Without some little defect here or there,
Be it in the head, or the hand, or the feet.'

He was sorry he had asked.

'You see, her *foot*. She is a changeling.'

Changelings were babies swapped at birth by faeries, he knew that. The girl was hardly a baby. Really, all the evidence was coming down on the side of his beloved wife being quite mad.

As it happened, Mrs Dewbank's prediction to her husband was correct. They were turned away at the door when they went calling three days later.

'She's not well,' Agatha apologised. She didn't like to say that the child had taken a violent and quite unreasonable, she thought, dislike to the old lady.

A child snatched away then given back is a child with enormous power. Even if she had not been ill, had not limped, whatever she wanted, of course, would have been done for her. As if she held a wand, her fairy godmother ran when she could walk to get something for her, scurried into shops, discovered places in the next town that she had never known. And bought from *JB Hifi, Dreamtime Bedding, Carpets Galore,* and especially *The Spiritual Bookshop* with its magic crystals. As requested, she painted the girl's bedroom purple, to set off the iron bed with its new leopard-skin throw. Posters of unicorns and dragons and witches were on the walls. And among all the new things were all the relics that Agatha had saved for her displayed on her shelves in the place of honour. Silver tap shoes, in different sizes, all now too small for her. And the unworn Doc Martens, which she said didn't fit.

Daphne dressed all in black, but Agatha had seen other girls dressed like her, the watered-down Goths who visited Wombat at the weekend. Red lips, black eyes, white matt faces and dressed in black witches' robes. Just a fashion. Like Daphne, they bought Alistair Crowley Tarot decks, second hand books on the occult. The local traders didn't mind black magic as long as it sold, and there was profit in the esoteric cards, books and runes that filled her daughter's shelves. She imagined Frank coming home, finding

Daphne, all her Tarot cards spread out on the floor, her red candles, her little hessian spell-bags to call up the faeries.

More and more, Agatha began to believe what the police said, that Frank had probably gone off with another woman. They had seen it before, they said.

And it wasn't as if the marriage had been smooth sailing, which they had often hinted.

Daphne watched documentaries – war crimes, murders, but especially child-abuse stories. She sat forward in her chair, taking in details of children held in cellars in Belgium, in England, in America.

Agatha found she dared not object to anything Daphne wanted to do, and if she wanted to watch these shows, perhaps it was as catharsis for the horrors she had been through.

But what exactly had she been through? When would she open up?

Once she had suggested they change the channel, but Daphne had snapped at her. Agatha looked at her then for the first time as if she was a stranger. She saw how desperately pale she was, how thin, how cold. Her voice was still a barely heard whisper, she still complained about dizziness and weakness.

Kurt believed in miracles.

Agatha and Kurt had talked about the situation on the phone or at the nursery when she could get out. Without her noticing it, he saw that Agatha had become a prisoner of her daughter. But Kurt did not want to confront Daphne. He knew if Agatha had to choose between them he would lose her.

He would rather wait, praying to God that it would pass, that he would once more be welcome at his lover's house.

And then, out of the blue it seemed, the Bible man's prayers were answered.

One day Daphne was helping her mother unpack the shopping, making sure she had remembered to get all her special orders from the butcher.

'Can I use that patch of rhododendrons and azaleas for bees?'

'Bees?'

'I've been watching a show about them. I know about setting up the hives and all that ...'

'Really?'

Was this the turning point, was Daphne moving on, developing new interests?

'And I meant to say something else. Bring Kurt here whenever you like. I think you need cheering up.' She smiled vaguely at Agatha's hesitation. 'Life goes on, doesn't it? And anyway, I'll be busy now setting up the bees. Maybe Kurt would like to help me? I could even set up a business. That would make you happy, wouldn't it?'

'All a mother wants is to see her daughter happy,' smiled her mother.

Yes, it was a miracle, declared Kurt.

Agatha was inclined to believe him.

The beehives were set up with Kurt's help, but the peace did not last for much longer than the time it took to finish the project. Had he outlived his usefulness to her?

Daphne's favourite spot was in Frank's recliner chair in front of the TV, a pile of subscriber magazines on her lap. There was always an article on eating disorders and Agatha had noticed her studying these closely.

'What do you think about these bulimics?' Agatha asked one night.

The girl did not look up from her magazine. 'I admire them.'

'*Admire*?'

'I mean, it would take such dedication.'

There was a moment's silence.

'You don't think I …?' She pitched the magazine across the room. 'Look, Mum, I've got something wrong with my blood. Are you saying I'm doing this to myself deliberately? Like them?'

'No, but …'

'No, but? But my own mother thinks I'm faking.' She jumped up with unusual energy and screamed in almost a normal voice from the doorway, 'How could you accuse me like that?'

'I didn't …'

'Well, you'll believe me when I die!'

And she slammed the door with surprising strength.

The miracle was over.

When she emerged, Daphne announced that she wanted cable TV.

Agatha had it connected.

But Agatha found it unsettling. Previously, if she could hear *The Simpsons*, it was around seven-thirty. If *Seinfeld* was on, it was around seven. If the talk shows were on, it was morning.

Now, she never knew what time it was – cable showed morning shows in the afternoon, midnight shows at midday. There were too many channels for Agatha to even read the program, anyway.

'You don't read it, Mum, you just flick.'

And that's what Daphne did, checking out what else was on, except when there was a good riveting show about disease or death. Nothing else held her interest as long.

The rhythm of the old TV shows, Agatha was surprised to realise (for she would not have called herself an avid watcher), had held an element of security.

This was one of the small things taken away from her now, under the new regime. A pattern had been established where she tiptoed around her daughter, who read, ate, slept, and watched TV twenty-four hours a day now, forever seeking out the same horrific shows.

'I'm watching, shhhsshhh …'

Agatha tried to ask her why she wanted to watch them, even asked her if something similar had happened to her. But she said she was too *traumatised* (she pronounced it with a US accent) to speak about it.

At night, Agatha started to take sleeping tablets to avoid nightmares where her own daughter was the central figure in the gruesome TV shows she watched.

Sometimes now Mr and Mrs Dewbank were permitted to join them for afternoon tea, but Daphne would studiously ignore them. On this occasion, the visitors had brought scones and jam and cream, and Mrs Dewbank was talking about the recessive features of certain humans. Giles shifted in his seat, hoping he wasn't going to be made an example of.

'They often have special powers, of course.'

'Like what?' snapped Daphne, her attention caught, her eyes flashing warily.

'Do you doubt me? I don't make mistakes about this.'

'Why, because you're a know-all genius?' she snarled.

'Darling …' soothed Agatha.

'It's her field of expertise,' put in Giles, hoping to placate.

'Yes, I do know everything – about certain creatures,' Mrs Dewbank said knowingly, placing her cup carefully back on its saucer. 'More than you would like to suppose.'

'I think you should leave now,' announced the girl.

In silence, the adults exchanged glances. The Dewbanks waited for her to speak, but Agatha didn't ask them to stay. Whatever the child wanted prevailed. Mr Dewbank knew there was no arguing. His own brother had two grown boys who lounged about watching TV and smoking dope, while he and his wife went out to work to support them.

It was no more sinister than that. Simply a case of a spoilt brat riding roughshod over a susceptible mother. He did not believe, as Magdala, insisted in bed that night, that the house had a dark past that had enabled a faery creature to seek it out.

In the end, it was the Channel 8 helicopter crew who found Frank. Disoriented, with a sprained ankle, about a hundred metres off the track. He had been sitting by a smoky campfire in the drizzling rain. The Channel 8 helicopter had spotted the smoke.

Daphne was asleep in front of the TV after finishing her favourite meal of liver and bacon, which she now made herself because Agatha always overcooked the liver.

one lamb's fry

250 grams of bacon

flour, salt, pepper

Soak the fry in cold salted water for half an hour. Cut into pieces one inch thick, wash well and dry thoroughly. Coat with seasoned flour. Remove rind from bacon. Heat frying pan and cook bacon in its own fat. If necessary, add more fat and cook liver ten minutes. (Daphne cooked hers for five.) *Place liver in centre of dish, bacon round edge. Pour over gravy made with drained-off fat, garnish with parsley.*

Agatha was eating spaghetti with pesto sauce and surprised herself by hardly pausing in her taking of the next mouthful as the news flash came on.

Frank hadn't realised that there was a hunt on for him. He was resting a twisted ankle before continuing and had run out of food. The film crew asked him to pose for the camera, eating his first food (a banana) for forty-eight hours. This was shown on the news flash. Unshaven man gorging on banana.

(Would the TV mention Daphne's disappearance too?) Agatha turned the volume down as low as she could, so as not to wake her.

Agatha at first did not recognise her husband, once neat, ordered, in that footage of a savage. His name was written on the screen as the moment was repeated in slow motion. Then the camera ran down his body to his ankle – bandaged. Beside his foot was the first-aid kit she knew he always carried.

The only question they asked him sounded to her more like a reprimand.

'How do you feel as an experienced bushwalker having a half million dollar search going on to reach you?'

He threw the banana skin on the fire before answering.

'I wish you'd never found me,' he said slowly.

Agatha felt tears in her eyes. If it had not been for her call to the police, the search would not have been started. She knew what he meant, though he did not tell the TV crew that he would not have minded dying. That he had been seeking out Daphne or death in the bush by walking alone. That he had begun to long for the spider-bite in the night, the twisted ankle.

Never found me ...

Agatha understood that he had not really been heading anywhere at all, that he had been walking, trekking, strolling, ambling, climbing, heading in only one direction, and that was away from himself, from his pain. Towards Daphne's body in its shallow grave. How could she have thought there had been another woman? The police had been so wrong about that.

When Frank had said he loved her, she knew it was true. There could never be any deceit on his part – other women's partners had affairs, led double lives, not Frank. Now, as she watched the TV image played over and over, she wanted to hold him close to her, to protect him.

She didn't realise that he was to become the media villain of the week, simply for speaking the truth. And she would see him as through the eye of the camera. Mad in his dirty clothes, unshaven. His intense eyes unwilling to meet its gaze.

And then, yes, their daughter's photo on the TV again. A five-year-old photo. The image of their daughter did not belong to them any more, but to the public.

And now a background briefing on the double family tragedy ...

Agatha switched off the TV.

A few days later there was a knock at the door. The girl opened the door to an unshaven man in a dirty parka, then shut it hard in his face. She started trembling. She called out for Agatha. 'Mum, there's a man at the door ...'

When Agatha opened the front door again, Frank was inspecting the shrubs on each side of the entry.

'They pong a bit, don't they – what are they?'

She threw her arms around his neck, laughing.

The girl hung back, watching him, until he became aware of her presence. He opened his arms to her. The girl hugged him, did not speak.

But she listened carefully to every detail of her parents' conversation as he came inside and sat at the kitchen table.

He showed her his pack, full of every gadget under the sun. He showed her some photos he had taken of his walks in the mountains. One was of a giant trout, still attached to his line.

'Fishing? Weren't you too upset for that after I was gone?'

Frank hesitated.

'Parents are supposed to be miserable when their daughter disappears,' she said, and there were tears in her eyes. 'What sort of father are you?'

Agatha stepped in. 'Dad was ... is ... broken-hearted. The heart breaks, but the body goes on, darling.'

Daphne turned to her father. 'I'm not well, you know, Dad,' she said, in her smallest voice.

He was watching her carefully, 'Yes, you look different.'

Suddenly she pulled up her T-shirt. 'Still got that tattoo you hated, Dad,' she laughed. The mermaid. Desired. Disruptive.

Frank was intrigued by Daphne's apparently instinctive ability to handle the bees, of which he was slightly fearful. He kept well away from them, and in private Agatha told him she was just as wary of them as he was. They let Daphne attend to them but apart from that, for the next few days, Frank did whatever Daphne wanted to do. More of the same – watching TV and cooking meat dishes. Agatha got her the ingredients from the butcher – kidneys, liver, pig's trotters, tongue.

Daphne now had enough energy to cook these things the way she liked them. She cooked curried kidneys, ox tongue, kidney pudding, liver and bacon delight. She offered these to Frank, and he ate them, as he was not a vego like Agatha, although he found them always a little underdone. As well as feeding him, Daphne also put herself in charge of keeping the TV news reporters away.

"I'll pretend I am your secretary.'

She answered their calls in a plummy telephone voice that they couldn't recognise as hers.

The TV was turned up so loud that Agatha and Frank lay awake in the room next door, unable to sleep. They heard the reporters cross-examine rape victims, the victims of assaults of all kinds.

'How did you feel when …?'

'Can you tell us what it felt like when …?

'Do you feel angry about …?'

'What would you like to say to the man who …?'

For Agatha, her daughter was all of these people, interviewed to the verge of tears. Agatha dreaded the day a journalist would arrive on their doorstep to interview her daughter about her 'experience.' How her life would 'never be the same again.'

Ah but it would be if Agatha had anything to do with it.

Agatha was dazed by the TV voices as she slumped back on her pillow. Frank groaned and placed soft putty plugs in his ears. She couldn't do that. Something might happen, the girl might call out to her.

Frank could still hear the TV.

Why did the girl have to watch all this tragedy?

Why did she have to watch it so loud?

But how selfish he was being, feeling his own pain, when it was his daughter who had been damaged. Still unable to talk about the pain. Still the distant look, the refusal to remember.

'It's in the past. I don't want to …'

'You'll have to go back to see the doctor.'

The girl pressed her lips together, closed her eyes, shook her head like a defiant four-year-old. 'Later, Dad, I'm not ready. You don't understand. I am the lost child. Like in the stories. Except no one came for me.'

'She limps … what's wrong with her foot?'

'She doesn't like to talk about it.'

It was the attacker, he told himself. But it looked as if one leg was shorter than the other, though it was hard to tell with those crazy platform shoes she wore all the time. Even her slippers were built-up boots made of fake fur.

Agatha started to cry, imagining the worst. Not knowing left room for all the media detail to agglomerate. Frank put his arms around her. His brother had one leg shorter than the other. Could such a thing happen after puberty? The body is still growing, of course. He supposed it could happen.

Was he being overly suspicious wondering why she no longer liked ginger, which used to be her favourite kind of jube? Or remember the name of her cat that had been run over?

That night, together, they watched *Invasion of the Body Snatchers*, where the Martian took the form of the woman's husband. He looked like him, acted like him. Was not him.

Interrogators formulated a question. Who won the baseball in a certain year, was that it? Something incomprehensibly American, but which he should know. The impostor didn't. Was it possible to discover a question like that, to catch her out?

Were the blank spots in her memory too convenient?

Frank suggested that they throw a party, invite her old school friends, distant cousins.

'I don't want to. They'll ask questions. I like it here with you. Just us.'

And so there was no party.

Frank then mentioned school. He supposed there was local one, though she was now over the age for compulsory schooling.

She showed no interest in returning to study. Her only outside interest seemed to be the bees. At least that got her out of the house.

To Frank, the house began to seem enchanted, as if the girl was casting a spell on Agatha. She had done little work on the project that used to feature in her emails to him, the *Womanly You* tour. At first she had written about working to tame the garden, about her passionate hatred of invasive blackberries, but then, apart from mentioning that lots of plants were self-seeding, she had stopped writing about the garden. It seemed to be taking care of itself, he observed, but wondered if *Womanly You* might require a little more effort than this.

'What happened to the Shakespeare's Garden idea?' he prodded her one morning over breakfast, looking out the window at the rampant jungle outside. It certainly seemed fertile to him, but in an unpleasant way.

'I seem to have got sidetracked.' She glanced at the daughter's booted feet, which were visible from the next room.

'I think you should get it going. It would be good for you …' He didn't finish his sentence.

Good for you to have an interest other than that girl.

They looked out the window together in silence. The garden was certainly bizarre. Frank was no gardener. Leave the Aussie bush in its natural state, gums and acacia, that was his idea of a garden. He did not recognise the herbs and flowers that were springing up all around them as if by magic, or know that some were totally out of season.

The sunlight, suddenly warming the soil after the claws of the blackberries had been withdrawn, must have altered nature's rhythm, thought Agatha. By now she recognised belladonna, with its pale purple flowers, the white feathery tops of hemlock, lily-of-the-valley, the tall purple spikes of monkshood, several oleander bushes which, though withered badly, were quick to recover, black-eyed Susan and above all, the azaleas enthusiastically climbing the house. (She hoped they weren't going to take over as badly as the blackberry had.)

127

'Come outside. I'll give you a garden tour,' she said to Frank, taking his hand. He stood up readily. He had to keep his legs moving after all that walking. Sometimes his legs started to move before he was awake. Walking would settle the muscles down, take his mind off his black ideas about the girl.

Outside they passed the twin sentinels at the front door, the dark green leaves of the shrubby savin junipers, with their flaking, red-brown bark. The pair in their planters were vigorously growing, as if competing with each other. It was unfortunate, she thought, that they had planted themselves there, for Frank was right – they gave off an unpleasant odour when bruised by traffic through the front door. She would have to plant them elsewhere.

They strolled around to the yew trees. Some had been damaged when the backhoe had uprooted blackberries whose tentacles had then dragged through the branches of the trees they had nearly strangled.

They walked around to the back of the house, pausing at the stained-glass windows of their daughter's room. Agatha showed him a new daphne bush that had sprung up, right outside the bedroom. She had shown it to the girl already. She had seemed pleased, but not surprised, to see her namesake paying homage to her.

Then she showed him the tall foxgloves, the Indian tobacco – she named all the plants for Frank. But she did not tell him what Mrs Dewbank had taught her – that every one of these plants that had sprung up of its own will was poisonous, and in the right dose, fatal.

'But where is your Shakespeare's Garden?' he asked, suddenly stopping their stroll to look at her. She said vaguely that the garden seemed to have other ideas.

'Should help the value of the house … when we move,' he ventured.

'Daphne wouldn't like a move. She needs stability. And the bees …'

They had avoided approaching the beehives.

'Ah yes, Daphne.' He shook his head.

'Anyone would think you were sorry she'd come back to us.' She wanted him to reach out for her, tell her it wasn't true, but he didn't.

'Maybe this is the time to say it, by the way,' he said quietly. 'I know about Kurt.'

There was suddenly ice in the space between the couple. Both held their breath, not wanting to admit it.

'Haven't seen him round,' he said eventually. 'I told you I'm not jealous. You need a bit of life in this place. Ask him round to dinner.'

This was not the scene that Agatha had dreaded. It was worse, an anti-climax, a denial of the importance of the relationship with Kurt. But how important was it, in fact? She was fond of him, but was that all?

'How did you know?'

'Heard it round town.'

Frank said that he wanted to see Agatha smile again, that he did not mind if it took another man to do it. The pressure of living out the nuclear family, reunited, a Happy Family again, was weighing on him heavily. He could no longer make love to Agatha. In bed, they hugged like Hansel and Gretel in the woods. If it took a lover to cheer her up, so be it.

'I'll call in and ask him,' said Frank.

'Don't you dare,' replied Agatha. 'I'll ask him myself.'

Also 'around town', Kurt had heard with dismay of her husband's return. Even so, Kurt was astonished to see Frank dropping Agatha off at the nursery. She waved to her husband as he drove off, then walked up to Kurt, smiling. She kissed him on the cheek as if nothing was wrong.

Kurt refused the invitation to dinner that Agatha then offered, issued, she told him, by her husband.

'What's going on?'

'He wants to meet you.'

'He *knows* about us?'

'Yes.'

'What is this, some kind of married game where I entertain you both at dinner with my pathetic emotions?' he asked. A bitterness she had not heard before was in his voice.

He blamed himself for not knowing about the possibility of this husband returning. But he had thought she did not want to talk about her past.

Agatha was holding out something to him. It was his toothbrush and a nose-dropper.

'You're returning all my things?'

He was flushed with anger.

'No, I ...'

He turned his back on her, hurried away to attend to a customer.

She tried to remember, as she watched his back, the classification of customers that they had laughed over together. She took a step towards the gilded man who had once filled her dreams, but he did not see her.

Daphne was taking a long bath, with oils and essences. By accident, Frank barged in on her. The bubbles were over the bath edge, slopping onto the floor. He told Agatha that he was sure she had seemed to be playing with some kind of fish, its silvery tail flicking back and forth near her feet. She had screamed hoarsely at him to get out, called him a pervert.

Perhaps, he thought, he was a pervert. He wanted to see her feet. She never walked barefoot, as she used to. Was her foot injured, perhaps infected, gangrenous?

'So Kurt didn't want to come?'

Frank was helping her clear some fallen branches around a fine pink flowering gum near the back fence, to clear up the rhododendron area where the beehives were set up. Daphne, of course, was inside, too weak to help.

'You seem to be sorry I'm not jealous,' he said, leaning over his work, not looking at her. They worked side by side, each looking at the branches, the ground, building up a pile of bark and branches between them with regular movements.

'Well, most people ...'

'I go away for months, after watching you leading a living death for years. Why?'

'We talked about it.'

'I wanted you to get on with living. With me around, we would always be talking about it. And you found Kurt to keep you company while I was gone.'

He stood up, but she kept on with her soothing movements, bending and lifting. 'And I'm supposed to throw a fit, forbid you to see him. Stop working for a moment and look at me.'

She stood up, reluctantly looking at him. She did not want to see hurt or anger in that face she still loved.

'Do you want me to go away again?'

'No, it's so important for Daphne ...'

'But you?'

'And me.'

She put her arms around him. She realised then that she loved two men.

'How can you stay with him when we love each other? You do love me, don't you?'

'Yes,' said Agatha.

She reached out to him, twined his long fingers in hers. She watched his tears, his anger, with regret. Agatha could not feel such passion any more. But she made love to him (and she did love his strong, tender passion) and he seemed to be consoled. Afterwards, though, when she said it was time to go back, it started again.

'Why do you have to go back?'

'Because it's time for dinner.'

'So simple? Just like that? I want a life with you, Agatha, don't you understand?'

He began to suspect she was actually making love with her husband, though he dared not ask her. He felt he was a plant whose sun was being blocked out by a brick fence. He could not share her. He sent her cards and letters, pleading.

You are my sun. Let's go away together ... start a family.

I can't share you.

I will die without you ...

These words seemed to arrive in Agatha's hands from a country far away, where customs were different. It was, in fact, just the country of the young.

He was moved to tears.

But she no longer wanted to be moved like that. She looked one last time at the most recent card, illustrated by two cartoon daffodils holding hands. Then she put it away in a tin of greeting cards with others of his, where it would exist for an indeterminate time in limbo between being kept and being thrown out on recycling day.

And how could he understand that she loved him but had no energy to start her life again? Daphne had drained it all.

Certain corners in the house were out of control. On the TV and stereo, dust was settling over the electronic equipment. Agatha refrained from dusting or tidying these corners, as Daphne would get upset if anything of hers was moved. She had tapes of TV shows labelled *talk show*, *medical drama*, *medical documentary*, *murders*. Doctor dramas, hospital dramas, and people on talk shows discussing variations of mental disturbance, the paranormal and illness.

Daphne kept her bedroom door shut now, and often when Agatha knocked to go in, she called out that she was busy, in a polite enough voice. When she pushed against the door, she found it was always jammed shut. Daphne liked to eat in there, takeaways delivered to the door – grey-fleshed chicken or pork ribs. Around the sink there was a build-up of chewed bones in her best cups and dishes.

This was the home that Frank had come back to – he had not been there to witness the slow, steady accretion of this detritus in the house, so slow that Agatha had hardly realised what was happening. 'Can't she clean up after herself?'

'But she's very ill, you know.'

He frowned, willing to consider an exoneration. 'What's wrong with her exactly?'

'Some kind of anaemia maybe.'

'We'll take her to better doctors –'

Suddenly they noticed Daphne standing at the door, holding a small, battered book to her chest. They wondered how long she had been listening.

'Are you talking about me again?'

'We were worried …'

'I hate people talking about me.'

'What are you reading, darling?'

Frank looked at his wife, again astonished at the way she papered over any cracks in the household dynamics.

'I found it on the shelf. *The Life of a Bee*, by Maurice Maeterlinck.'

They both smiled at this healthy interest of hers, which got her outside into the garden, moving around. She never asked them for help now that the hives had been set up.

'The sun's out, Daphne. Why don't you try to get out – you could read it on the bench out near the hives.'

'Yes,' smiled Daphne, 'I was just going to do that.'

She drifted out into the garden, and her parents tried to contain their optimism.

'Exercise, at least,' said Frank.

In silence, they watched her through the window. The sun was shining on the large area of azalea and rhododendron bushes which seemed to spread by the day. The old bench would be quite comfortable to sit and read, and the girl limped towards it with her book. A happy picture of a normal girl, reading a book about bees, sitting among the rhododendrons of her parents' house. Agatha felt at that moment as if she had been granted three wishes by a fairy godmother.

Her child was back.

Her husband was back.

And she had a house in the country.

What could go wrong? She hadn't even messed up the third wish, as they did in fairy tales.

But Frank was still battling his feelings that this girl was not their daughter at all. He tried to tell himself that all parents feel that to some degree when their lovely child reaches the hormonal hell of puberty – he had read that in some magazine. This was, perhaps, just an extreme case of those feelings of non-recognition, exacerbated by the years apart, and by the poor child's trauma. He had read somewhere else that bringing it all out in the open was good for everyone, no matter how painful, but he wasn't so sure that digging up the past was always a good thing. Getting old, he felt, would be easier if you lived with someone who had the same memories as you, so that the past did not have to be raked through. For this reason he wanted to stay with Agatha, even if it meant her having a lover. It was as if the house itself was depleting his sexual energy. And having Daphne in the house was forcing that other memory of loss and nightmare to lose its clarity. He tried to explain this to Agatha, to see if it was the same for her.

'Like double exposures,' he said.

Catalogue items materialised, boxed and complete with invoices made out to Frank. Unlike Agatha, their daughter did not cancel after receiving the Free Gifts. Agatha's free gifts had included a calendar with international time settings, a key ring shaped like a tiny pocketknife and a radio shaped like a phone. These were hers, just for inspecting the company's products.

Cookbooks, saucepan sets, instant tans and weight-loss programs, instant language programs (*learn while you sleep*) – even a beach house in Queensland, 'fully serviced'. All had been resisted.

Agatha's frugal lifestyle had changed since the girl's return. Frank could not reprimand her for her generosity, but the girl was being spoilt with clothes, CDs, computer games and endless catalogue purchases. Agatha let her subscribe to anything she liked.

Making up for lost time, he tried to tell himself.

Still, Daphne was not a visitor. She would have to study or at least register for a job.

They would have to discuss finances.

The family had just watched *The Wizard of Oz* on TV, because Daphne had wanted to. The females were talking about killing the wicked witch, as Frank was nodding off on the couch, killing the wicked witch ... and he woke with a start, because suddenly the wicked witch had his daughter's face.

'How can you kill a witch anyway?' scoffed Agatha, when the ads came on.

'Well, they don't drown, do they?' said Frank, trying to rouse himself from his sudden vision.

'You can burn them,' said Daphne, from her position on his recliner. 'That's the best way.'

She knew about disease, he thought, and she knew about death.

Frank was sitting in the kitchen, eating bananas and reading, with fearful recognition, an article in the paper about the effects of an over-active thyroid.

A woman believed her two daughters were possessed by demons. She contacted a local cult, who agreed to organise an exorcism. A medical social worker suggested such delusions were typical of hyperthyroidism.

The patient complains for days about having a sore neck.

Frank felt his swollen neck.

She was unable to sleep.

Frank yawned.

And she was losing weight ...

Frank felt his ribs.

... though she was always ravenous ...

Frank counted the bananas he had eaten.

This condition is known as thyrotoxicosis, or Graves' disease. It causes paranoid behaviour and psychic disturbances.

This woman believed her daughters had the devil's eyes, and tried to force them to attend the exorcism. The social worker reported her delusions ...

Delusions? After the accident the doctor had told him he had an over-active thyroid, and not to worry about how thin he was, how ravenous. It was not a tapeworm, he had assured him. Frank had taken the medication for a while, but, not considering the affliction serious, he had stopped.

What if he was imagining all kinds of devilish intentions about his daughter, just because he was ill? He resolved then to be more assiduous in taking his medication.

He would try to make it up to her, to Agatha, somehow.

How mundane modern medicine renders life, after all, he thought. Relieved.

There were dramas now each time Agatha saw Kurt. He begged her to go away with him, to move away from Frank. From her daughter. To start again. This struggle did not stop them making love each time they saw each other. In bed, he was still her golden man.

Agatha was trying to work on her next column. *When mulching, be sure not to lay the dressing too close to the stems of plants as this can cause rot ...*

A phone call from the hospital interrupted her.

'We've got Mr Kurt Ward here, who gave your name as next of kin.'

'Kurt – has there been an accident?'

'He wants to see you.'

'What happened to him?'

'He said he was working with the wattles, and he's allergic to them, so he took a dose of nasal inhalant to prevent an attack. But then he just collapsed. Eden, his boss, was there – she said she thought he was dead. She called the ambulance and we were able to revive him. But now he's relapsed ...'

Sitting by the hospital bed was an elderly woman dressed in black, with an old fashioned cloche hat pulled down over her neat grey hair. She did not look up at Agatha. They both watched Kurt from opposite sides of the bed.

His eyes were closed and he did not seem to be aware that she was there. His face was pale, the skin around his nose and mouth was red and raw, as if it had been burnt, and he was breathing through an oxygen tube. Suddenly the woman spoke, still keeping her head down, her eyes, Agatha saw now, on a small Bible. Her accent was a harsher version of Kurt's. 'I am his aunt. Next of kin. We ship body to our country for church funeral.'

Fighting back tears, Agatha took his hand. It was damp and limp in hers.

'You go now,' the woman ordered.

Cheated of a last farewell to Kurt, even at the graveside, Agatha sobbed out her pain to Frank. Calmly, Frank listened to the details, holding her gently. It all seemed to be happening far away in another world. Her body was reacting, however. She had a sickly sense of nausea. She longed for Frank to want her passionately once more.

That night she dreamt that Kurt was on a raft, naked, gilded with gold dust, drifting away from her on a cold dark lake.

She woke in a sweat, and in the dawn light, watched Frank sleeping. So fragile, he seemed.

She was sure he was getting thinner each day, though he was always hungry, and enjoyed the meat dishes Daphne made for herself and him. But she had never noticed before that fine tremor of the hands. His eyelids were drawn back, making his eyes seem permanently startled. He often appeared to be staring at her, and at their daughter.

Examining them.

Daphne cooked leg of lamb so that it was blood-red inside, but cooked on the outside. She served Frank the cooked slices, reserving the bloody insides for herself. Agatha ate the roast vegetables cooked in a separate pan.

'I love your cooking, Daph.'

The girl was pleased. 'I can make a lamb curry tomorrow – I'll put tofu in yours, Mum.'

Frank put one arm around Daphne and the other around Agatha. He must fight those delusions about his daughter. As Agatha rested her head against his chest, she felt his heart skip a beat, then give a great thump. It was as strong as if it was in her own chest. She looked him in his staring eyes.

'Frank, what's wrong with you?'

'I'm taking medicine, it'll work soon.'

'What is it?'

'Nothing. It's just a thyroid problem.' He fished out a bottle of tablets and shook them under her nose. 'See? The medical profession is taking good care of me.'

He had to see the doctor again for more tablets, so he decided to take Daphne with him. He told Agatha he would like her to see a doctor about the limp. Agatha was against it.

'She doesn't need any pressure,' she kept saying. 'Not yet. Anyway, she's always limped.'

'What are you talking about? She used to dance so well.'

For a moment, he distrusted his own memory.

'Why are you looking at me like that? Do you think I'm making it up?'

One of them must be wrong. But which one?

Frank started as a tour guide for city folk up in the bush for the day. He gave them coffee and cake before setting out into the bush, carried salt and matches for leeches, first-aid kit, compass and ferried them to the start point where necessary. It was a lackey's job, he knew, for someone who had walked the GDT. Or most of it.

He told them never to break the fundamental rule of bushwalking by walking alone. Risking the twisted ankle that meant shelter could not be reached by nightfall. Risking the fatal bite from the spider in the sleeping bag with no one to help.

Soon, he wanted to run his own business. He knew the best walking routes. He would advertise in Europe. He wished he would get better soon. He was often short of breath, and the tremor in his hands sometimes made his handwriting look like an old man's. The doctor had said the anti-thyroid drugs would take about eight weeks to work. Then he would always have to take a maintenance dose. He ran his fingers over the smooth lump on his neck. Surgical removal of a goitre was a possibility, but he had always feared anaesthetics. He tried not to dwell on his minor condition. Instead, he played computer games with his daughter to get her away from the TV gore. But they were just as bad – killing and maiming. You would think, it seemed to him, that a girl who had been through her pain would want to forget about it all.

But what, exactly, had she been through?

He wished she would take some exercise, but she was always too weak, too pale, too dizzy to help Agatha in the house, to even stand up most of the time. Except to tend the bees. So deprived, he supposed. Even if she was bunging it on, let her lap up the home life she had missed.

And he did like her cooking.

Daphne announced that she had seen the werewolf from her window, two nights in a row. In the middle of the night. She told them calmly. She had not called them, she didn't want to frighten them.

They went around to the window of her bedroom, and saw that the bracken had been trampled down and a few branches of the daphne bush were snapped.

Then it happened.

Agatha's periods were rare these days; she had assumed she was in the menopause, had taken no precautions. But there were other signs. It explained the nausea she was feeling. There was no doubt about it, she was over four months pregnant, the doctor told her. She prodded at her belly, already tight and full.

'But how could you not have known?' the doctor cooed, stroking and prodding. 'I would say by the size that it's closer to five months actually. You can start over again.' She did not say what she really thought. That she wished Agatha better luck this time with her offspring.

The energy of the house had drained him of all desire, so Frank knew that the baby could not be his. But he would pretend it was, he said, holding Agatha gently in his arms. Yes, he would claim this interloper for his own.

He too secretly wished for better luck this time. Perhaps it was he after all who had the bad bloodline. At night he sometimes dreamt he was the werewolf.

'Let's have a dinner to celebrate,' he said.

They told Daphne, who seemed delighted, and offered to cook a special meal. 'Do you like spicy rice?' she asked Agatha.

She assured her that would be a lovely change.

Daphne looked glad to have a little sister, or brother.

Everything, it seemed, was settling down.

So that night, they sat down to the candle-lit table that Daphne had covered with a purple velvet cloth. She had set it with Agatha's best silver and bunches of azaleas and rhododendrons.

'My bees love them.'

'They're beautiful.'

Daphne had prepared classic *boudin*, she said, a French dish.

one quart of fresh blood

one pound of onions

one pound of finely chopped fresh pork fat

a cup of cream

a handful of breadcrumbs

salt, pepper, fennel and chopped parsley

intestines

Wash the intestines thoroughly, steep with salt.

Stand the blood in another crock, allowing to cool

Boil the onions.

Mix all this with blood.

Fill the lengths of intestine with the mixture, tying up one end first, leaving enough length after you have filled it to tie it up.

Stack the boudins in a cauldron. Cover with cold water, bring to a gentle simmer, and cook without allowing water to boil.

When you prick them with a fork, and no blood comes out, they are sufficiently cooked. Take off heat and allow to cool.

Cut off lengths of cold boudin. Broil them on an oiled rack with the grill as hot as possible, until the skin becomes hot and caramelised.

Sauté some bacon in a pan with a little of the pork fat.

Add cream.

Serve.

Daphne looked particularly pale that night as she brought the blood pudding out and placed it proudly on the table, then poured out the wine into Agatha's best glasses.

For Agatha there was a wild rice dish, with greens, onions, ginger and a lot of fresh chilli.

'You said you liked it spicy, Mum.'

They raised their glasses.

'To the new baby,' said Frank, and all three drank.

Frank eyed the blood pudding Daphne placed on his plate, his mouth watering. He pricked the skin with his fork. Blood oozed out.

The black rice was spicier than Agatha was used to and she had trouble eating it but did not want to offend her daughter. She drank lots of water and wine to wash down the burning taste. She suspected she had bitten into a lump of chilli. Frank finished his *boudin*, asked for more.

This was followed by ice cream and fudge sauce, the coolness very welcome on Agatha's palate.

Daphne jumped up immediately to clear away and insisted on washing all the dishes. Then she said she would go to bed early as cooking all day had made her very tired. How gracious she was capable of being, thought Agatha, as she watched the thin waif leave the room.

In the middle of the night, Agatha woke with violent stomach cramps. She rushed into the bathroom, vomited her entire dinner, then a greenish substance with a strange ether-like odour.

The doctor arrived, a locum they did not know, and said that she did not need an emetic. There was nothing left in the stomach. He made her drink a litre of milk, to relieve the gastric irritation.

'What on earth have you eaten?'

'Rice, greens ...'

The doctor clucked his tongue. 'Giardia. It's in the water. That would explain it.'

He left her with some tablets to be taken every two hours to stop dehydration, assuring Agatha she would feel better in the morning.

All night, Agatha lay next to a snoring Frank. By morning, after a night of no sleep, Agatha had started shaking and sweating.

She got up and tiptoed out. She barely made it to the toilet seat before she was attacked by waves of dizziness and nausea, shooting pains and flashing lights.

Then she looked at her thighs.

Blood.

She could see blood, yet she was too dizzy, too weak to call out. She concentrated on breathing deep and hard to maintain consciousness and she thought of the labour room, of the birth of Daphne. The pain was the same. She knew she was losing this baby.

Frank found her still sitting there an hour later, slumped, shivering and cold. He saw the blood, he knew what had happened, and was surprised to feel a great burden lift from his shoulders. In silence, he put her to bed with the electric blanket turned up high, wanted to ring for the doctor. Agatha stopped him.

'No point,' she said.

He felt her forehead. It was cooler.

Though Frank would never say it, of course, he felt a wave of relief that this had happened. He would have tried to love the baby, her baby, but now he could concentrate on solving that other problem. The problem of Daphne.

From now on, he would take over the cooking.

It is nearing Christmas. He buys some Santa Spray. Looks for a reaction. She does not seem to remember it being significant.

He prods. 'Remember when you went to the shop?'

Still no reaction.

'Do you remember what you went down to buy?'

Suddenly she picked up the can and aimed it just over his head, spraying it at him, laughing at her joke.

Then she narrowed her eyes, holding the can up threateningly on a level with his face. 'That's what you do if a man grabs you in the street. You spray them right in the eyes.'

'Did you do that when he grabbed you?' he asked quickly.

She put the can down. 'I told you. I'm not ready yet,' she said firmly.

Frank had a sudden impulse to reach out and throttle her to make her talk. Instead, he pitched the can hard against the wall, which made her smile with satisfaction.

At about three o'clock on Friday afternoon, Frank told Daphne that he had made an appointment for her to see the locum. At first he told her it was about her weight. Then he said it was about her limp. She refused to go with him. She claimed she didn't like men touching her. Would wait until the woman doctor was back.

The second time he told her he had an appointment for four o'clock and she said she couldn't go because that was when her favourite TV show was on. He said the woman doctor was back and she could miss the show. She told Agatha she felt too dizzy to go. Frank backed down.

The third time he told her the appointment was with a counsellor to help her over her 'experience'. She hugged the pillow she was holding tighter, shook her head and looked at Agatha.

Agatha said she wasn't ready yet.

And so she continued tending the bees, watching TV and eating meat dishes she cooked herself (which Frank would no longer touch). Frank cooked plain rice and veggie dishes for himself and Agatha – he no longer felt like eating meat either. Agatha seemed to be recuperating, but still had trouble with her digestion.

He bought a walking machine for Daphne and put it in front of the TV. It stayed in its plastic wrap. She seemed to have sporadic energy and would go out to tend her bees among the azaleas and rhododendrons, now house-high, every day.

She changed all the posters on her bedroom walls. The fairies and dragons came down, up went more Gothic art – smeared blood-like lipstick on black-clad vampires, posters for cult movies about the undead. She lived by candlelight in her own cave, refusing to turn on the electric light or to let Agatha clean up.

Silence and sullen refusal were her weapons.

To come back from the dead is to have total power over the living.

The last time he made an appointment, Agatha was out shopping. He made sure of that. Frank told Daphne to get in the car; she refused. He took her hand and she screamed at him. Her face was covered with black eye make-up, red lipstick. She told him that she hated him. He didn't let go. She was not physically strong, and he pulled her towards the car.

Two kids on bikes stopped to snigger at the drama, at the man trying to get the witch into the car. He managed to get the seat belt around her in the back seat and thanked God for central locking.

He had a barrage of tests lined up for her. First was an examination of her limp. Was it an injury or a congenital malformation that he knew his own daughter did not have?

Then a DNA test. On the road he looked at her in the rear-view mirror and her eyes shone red at him. She screamed foul words. She loathed him.

She would tell Agatha, she threatened, who would kick him out and then they could be happy again. She wished he were dead. He kept driving with no apparent reaction.

Then she appeared to soften, weep.

'You don't know what it was like, what I've been through.'

He winced, but then the anger took over again. He was driving too fast, he knew that, as he hurtled along the narrow winding road that separated the house from the town, from the doctor.

At first he didn't hear the siren because of her screaming. Then he saw the flashing lights in the rear-view mirror but his only thought was to reach the doctor. After so many abortive attempts he at last had her in the car, on the way, and now this. He would explain to the cops later but for now his foot hit the accelerator.

The little car had a lot of power but they were catching him up. He lost his nerve and veered off the road on a tight curve, left the bitumen, tore through a wire fence, uprooting the posts, and came to a halt in a paddock with a lone and startled horse.

Two cop cars, one each side of him. They were young, smiling, high on the adrenalin of the chase. It was a game to them, maybe their first chase in their short careers.

'Where's the fire, mate?'

Frank felt as if he was in a movie.

Daphne screamed at them.

'He's trying to abduct me!'

She jumped out of the car, made a bolt for it. The taller cop blocked her way.

Frank pulled the other one aside.

'Hey, aren't you …?'

'She is not my daughter. She is a parasite. I want to know where she comes from, why she is here, and where my real daughter is. I'm taking her for tests.'

'Tests?'

They looked at each other.

'Isn't she …?'

'Just a moment, sir.'

They radioed in. The girl was the missing *milkbar girl*, the one who had turned up out of the blue. The one they had wanted to interview, but was too disturbed as yet. All was in order. Of course she was his daughter.

Why else would she be living with such a loony? Look at him, he was thin and his eyes were protruding as if they were going to pop out. They would have liked to take him in but the station said to let him go with a warning. He was the bushwalker man. It might hit the papers.

So they told him to take his daughter home again.

'But forget the tests. The station will help you get any test you like when the doctors say she's ready.'

The two cops put her into the back of the car, Daphne compliant, smiling at them. They watched the car do a U-turn, drive away.

'Shame about that girl.'

'Yeah. There should be a law against loonies procreating.'

On the way back Daphne sat in the back seat with her arms folded. Only once she spoke to him, triumphantly. 'See, I am the undead and I rule the world. I am here to stay.'

Children always find a witch's house.

Ding dong.

The children crept up to the windows and saw Gothic images from horror movies decorating the walls, a naked girl dancing by the candlelight.

Ding dong.

Frank waited until the next time Daphne was in the garden tending the bees among the rhododendrons. Then he went into her room. Neither of them had been permitted to enter for some time. There had been the werewolf incident where the crushed daphne had been displayed, but that had been an exception. Such an exception that it made Frank wonder if there had been a reason, a plan, which involved them witnessing the crushed daphne bush, evidence of, if not a werewolf, at least an intruder.

The room was dark, the blinds drawn. The vampire posters had been further decorated with red lipstick, simulating blood oozing from the corners of their mouths. He opened her drawers – cigarettes, broken cassette tapes. He picked them up, turned them over, pocketed a few of them. He wanted to be sure. And then, in the back of the drawer, what looked like a new packet of lollypops.

Curious, he extracted them.

Agatha saw Frank come out of the girl's room with something in his hand. 'She doesn't like you to go in there.'

He put the packet on the kitchen table in front of Agatha. They could see her outside in the garden.

At first Agatha did not recognise the object on the table, wrapped in plastic. Delicate orange and white, nicely designed and thin. Then it dawned on her. Thin, this object of worship by junkies. Who made themselves thin in its likeness ... the neat pack of four syringes.

One missing.

Frank called the girl in from the garden. She pretended not to hear him. He called again and she came inside.

The needles were on the table.

'Where did they come from?' she asked.

Frank told her.

'I don't know how they got there,' she said.

'Maybe it was the werewolf at the window,' Frank said bitterly.

The girl looked at Agatha, seeking her support. But Agatha had her head in her hands.

The girl waited before answering him. 'It's not what you think,' she said, in her weak voice. 'Anyway, if you go snooping round in people's rooms ...'

'Yes?'

'You deserve what you find, that's all,' she said with a half-smile.

Frank threw the syringes in the bin.

'Is that all?' said the girl, her face blank, her eyes cold. A stranger to them.

Agatha looked up at her. 'Tell us, darling, we're worried. We can get help for you ...'

She laughed at them. 'It's not what you think,' she repeated scornfully, and turned away, limping more than ever, then closing the door of her room quietly behind her.

Agatha rang the doctor, the same one who had seen Daphne at the hospital. She told her what had happened. The doctor was surprised.

'We checked for that at the hospital. She didn't show any signs of addiction – I don't see how she could have used the drug while she was under observation. We took all her things. The low blood count didn't indicate … Unless … '

'Unless?'

'Do you think you could convince her to come in again to stay overnight?'

Surprisingly, Daphne agreed.

'Then you'll know I'm not some pathetic junkie,' she said to them. 'Fancy my own parents not believing me.'

The same blood tests, the same result. The doctor spared no information from Daphne this time.

'Your blood count is so low,' said the doctor, 'that I would have to say it is incompatible with life.'

Daphne smirked. 'Really?' She seemed delighted.

'But there's one strange thing. The total blood count is down, the reticulocyte … '

Agatha looked lost.

'I mean the red blood cell count is up.'

Daphne tossed her head. 'So you can't explain it?' Frank saw that same look of triumph he had seen in the car. 'That's rather inept of you isn't it, doctor?'

There was a sneer in the title she used. 'Of course there is one explanation,' she added, holding back her anger.

Frank and Agatha sat forward. Daphne drew back, looked sceptical.

'Another stab in the dark?'

'But I can't be sure until you stay overnight.'

The next morning, Frank and Agatha were back at the hospital.

Further tests after twenty-four hours seem to have convinced the doctor that whatever her theory was, it was right. 'I believe I know what's going on,' she said carefully. 'But perhaps Daphne would like to explain it herself?'

Daphne looked into the doctor's eyes, attempting to stare her out, but then suddenly dropped her gaze, seeming to panic as she continued to speak.

'I've seen another case like this – with the syringes used in the same way.'

Daphne stood up. 'Let's go,' she said, tugging at Agatha's sleeve.

'Yes, you go if you like, Daphne,' suggested the doctor impatiently. And with surprising energy, her foot not dragging as much as it usually did, Daphne seemed to fly across the room. She charged out, slamming the door after her.

Agatha wanted to follow her but Frank and the doctor restrained her.

'But how will she get home?'

'The same way she arrived the first time.'

'It's better if she's not here.'

'How can you say that?'

'Because Daphne is doing this to herself.'

'How do you mean?'

Agatha listened in horror as the doctor explained that Daphne was using the syringes to bleed herself, then squirting the blood into the toilet to get rid of it.

'But why?'

'Drawing blood makes her feel calm, perhaps. It's a neurotic coping mechanism. That explains the low blood count,' said the doctor, then added as if to herself, 'and the high red cell count with no blood loss found.'

'But …'

'An invalid can rule a household. It's a great power trip for her. And then there's the pleasure she gets out of making a fool of everyone – not only you, but me, the other doctors.'

Agatha saw again the nine-year-old lying in a bath of bloodied water, seeming to enjoy it. Was it her early menarche that had set up the girl's preoccupation with bleeding and blood? Turned her into her own private vampire?

'And she needs, perhaps, to test your love for her.'

It came as a shock to Frank to realise that he had been so concerned with setting tests for her that he had missed seeing that she was perhaps doing the same thing.

Setting tests of their love for her.

Mrs Dewbank lowered her binoculars.

'Anyway, Giles, I'm just asking you to consider it as a possibility. That the child is a past soul who has died violently and has returned to look for a lost mother. And as for the miscarriage – I'm sorry but I saw that too.'

He rolled his eyes. 'What miscarriage?'

'Really, dear, you are a trial. One does not ask for the second sight, it really is quite a burden to those who have it. You know that pair of dwarf *juniperus Sabina* by the front door?'

'That smelly thing?'

'Yes.'

'I saw the precious girl fiddling around with that with a razor blade the afternoon before Agatha was ill.'

'So?'

He reflected that this incident could have been seen out the window with the aid of binoculars, with no need of the second sight. But he said nothing.

'The entire plant is toxic – *savin* is the other name, and in ancient times it was used to cause abortions. The only problem was that it was usually fatal to the mother also. It wasn't just food poisoning she had, when she cooked that special hot chilli dinner – so much chilli was needed to cover the bitter taste of the chopped savin greens. She was very polite to eat it.'

She passed him the binoculars. 'You can see yourself. The bush on the left is chopped back. She would have used little bits of woody twig as well as the leaves.'

'But she told us it was food poisoning, she vomited.'

'Yes, and a splendid thing that she had that reaction. If she hadn't vomited, she would have been dead from respiratory failure in ten hours. As it is she will probably have trouble with her kidneys for the rest of her life.'

Giles put down the binoculars, paused a moment. 'Are you going to tell her?'

'She would choose not to believe me.'

Giles suddenly had what he was proud to note was a very creative thought.

'You think she had something to do with Kurt's death too, don't you?'

'Of course. The nose-dropper. I saw her with the window of her bedroom open, picking berries from that daphne bush. Highly poisonous, of course. Perhaps a syringe into the berry, then into the nose dropper.'

'Really, darling, you should be writing Agatha Christie novels.'

'Why thank you, my dear,' she beamed.

He had not meant it as a compliment.

'But no,' she continued, 'my explanation is more metaphysical. There is only one way to get rid of this lost soul. Her spirit will no longer be attracted to the house if Agatha gets rid of her things, the shrine of her bedroom. Then she can go back to the ethereal world. She has been waylaid by the lower spirits on her way to heaven, is unable to let go of this earthly realm, but we could help her.'

'How?'

'You could set fire to the house, Giles. To her bedroom.'

Giles fiddled nervously with the scar behind his ear.

When the parents had returned from the hospital they found Daphne tending calmly to her bees as if she had never left. 'Took her long enough. She's so dumb, that doctor. I'm still smarter than her …'

Yet they found her seemingly calmer, almost resigned to the fact that her ruse had been exposed. Whatever the motivation had been, it seemed that the girl had abandoned the habit. Soon she had a little colour in her cheeks, began to put on weight and even her voice became stronger.

So Agatha had more energy to deal with *Womanly You.* If her editor found out that after all this time her garden was thriving with poison plants instead of nicely cottagey ones and Shakespeare's flowers, Agatha knew she would lose her contract.

So she rang to suggest a new concept.

Mrs Dewbank was at him again the next day.

'Yes, as I keep telling you, the best thing is to burn down her room with all her things in it. To release her spirit, to force it to let go of the material world.'

Giles looked over his shoulder to make sure no one was listening. He guessed what was happening. He excused himself and rang the airline to bring their departure date forward. She had finished her work on *homo aquaticus,* was moving on to her next book. She had finished her obsession with all things fishy, he could see, and was feeling around for the next theory. Which by the sound of it – burning bedrooms, wandering spirits and fires – would make the *homo aquaticus* book look quite tame.

She called out to him. 'And then of course, there are the bees.'

He came back in to the room, intrigued at this new angle in spite of himself. 'It's just a hobby, isn't it?'

But he knew she was going to twist that innocent occupation around too. He observed himself, aware that her mind fascinated him still. 'You've finished the major work, dear, haven't you?'

'Yes,' she beamed. 'You always know, don't you, you're so clever.'

And she kissed him, caressed his ears and the twin scars behind them.

'Would you like a spa, dear?' he murmured.

It had been a while.

'Splendid idea. And ah yes, the bees. The Greeks, of course, knew that the honey of bees that were fed on azaleas, rhododendrons, oleander or dwarf laurel – all in her patch – is poisonous.'

And Giles went to organise the spa, deciding not to add valerian this time.

The wind was a wild westerly, whipping around the house. A farewell afternoon tea of scones and jam and cream was set up for Mr and Mrs Dewbank, as it was the day before their departure. They were late. Daphne and Agatha were at the table, Frank was reading *Dr Jekyll* by the fire.

'They won't come, you know,' said Daphne, with satisfaction.

'She said she would. They're going back to Bath tomorrow.'

The girl rolled her eyes. 'The wind is in the west,' she said.

'So?'

'Well, she arrived when the wind was in the east, didn't she?'

'Really darling, I always knew you read too much Mary Poppins. Is that why you don't like Mrs Dewbank, because she reminds you of her?'

Daphne thought for a moment. 'But I *do* like her. Look,' she added, and with a flourish produced a plate of yellow cakes from under a cloth. 'I cooked these honey cakes specially for her.'

'Can we taste them?'

'No', said the girl quickly, 'they're just for *her*.'

Frank was sitting in silence, listening to this conversation, knowing that he would have to go away again. Knowing that he would never again eat anything this girl cooked.

Mr and Mrs Dewbank rang to say they were at the airport already, were going home early, were sorry they couldn't come.

Daphne picked up her honey cakes, secreted them in a little cellophane bag. 'I'll post them,' she said.

Agatha looked out the window as she was clearing up after the afternoon tea of scones that she had made herself, and imagined Mrs Dewbank sailing up into the sky, the west wind lifting her by her umbrella higher and higher into the air, her giant carpetbag in her other hand.

But then, what would have happened to Mr Dewbank?

Tired of waiting to hear from her, Agatha finally rang her editor.

'We do hope you haven't done too much work on the Shakespeare concept.' Agatha braced herself. 'The results from our readers are in and it seems the concept is a bit too highbrow after all, as I predicted. A little corner, perhaps, of Shakespeare's flowers, but the whole thing – his poems and all … we don't go with it.'

'How about the new concept?'

'Ah yes, well that was a surprise. Common poisons in the garden … rhododendron, daphne – amazing really, everything seems to be poisonous.'

'How did it rate with the readers?'

'Amazingly well. It seems there are thousands of *Womanly You* readers out there who want to learn about poisonous plants, and even how to use them in the kitchen – just for historical interest, of course, as we'll stress. Thousands of women in their kitchens, serving out food every night want this secret, powerful knowledge, just imagine … it's really hit a chord with them. Such power in the hands of the most downtrodden, kitchen-tied wife. We'd have to legal it, of course. I mean, we wouldn't want to be charged with conspiracy to murder, would we? Work on a title, dear, for the tour … and it's on. *Dangerous friends in the garden* … oh yes, that's good. *Dangerous friends …*'

Sounds like an Agatha Christie title, thought Agatha, seeing a budget for renovations, the sign already out the front of *Agatha Springs* advertising *Womanly You* Tours.

Exotic and fascinating plants (it did not say poison).

Hosted by Agatha Hock, of Happy Hock fame.

Best not to mention the poisons.

After all, imagine the reaction if people knew that all the lady cottage gardeners, readers of *Womanly You,* were becoming expert in the everyday plant poisons at hand in their gardens, these women in charge of the kitchens around the country, happily murdering at every meal. Imagine, the more women controlled the kitchen, the more they would be feared. It could include recipes, perhaps, for poisonous teas? Salads of chopped rhubarb leaves?

Agatha's entire gardening following arrested for conspiracy to murder?

No. Very bad for circulation.

Womanly You chose a more discreet path. Agatha's new column would be called simply *Cottage Garden Medicine.* It had a natural place in *Womanly You.*

Poisoning. Simply an extension of the role of the cook, the nurturer, the mother figure – Kali, dispenser of Life and Death.

One day the miser felt an impulse to inspect the love of his life, his gold. He got a shovel to dig it up. His shovel soon hit something hard and he cried out in anticipation. He got down on his hands and knees and scraped the dirt away, tearing his fingernails. Soon the dirt was cleared. But what was this?

He cried out in despair. Someone had taken his gold and replaced it with a huge block of useless bluestone, heavy and valueless.

In her half sleep, Agatha saw the miser who could have let that stone stay buried. Could have chosen deception and a type of happiness indistinguishable from the real thing.

She woke to the sound of the magpies, carolling sweetly now, welcoming her to the new day. The sunlight through the bedroom window made the air shimmer. The blue bedspread, the yellow curtains, even the sparkling spring water in its glass by the bed radiated an otherworldly light.

What was so different about this morning? When Frank had told her last week that he was going away bushwalking again and didn't know when he would be back, it had seemed natural, almost pre-ordained and she had not protested.

And she knew now that it had been the best for all. The girl, the house itself, seemed to settle into unearthly calm as soon as he had left, as if the house itself had wanted to expel him.

She thought again of her three wishes.

She had the house.

She had her daughter back, in spite of her sister's gloomy prediction.

Only the third one had not come true, as both the men in her life were now gone. But she should not be too greedy.

Outside the window, she could see the girl tending her bees in the pink and red blooms of azaleas and rhododendrons that were spreading from the hives, threatening to cover the entire house. Agatha watched Daphne move from hive to hive. She was moving with new strength this morning, and barely seemed to be limping at all.

Full of new energy, Daphne had again cooked her sticky yellow honey cakes, and again, Agatha had not been allowed to eat them.

'The recipe's not quite right yet,' Daphne had explained.

Frank had his secret that he would never share with Agatha. In the girl's bedroom, the day he had discovered the syringes, he had found something else.

He had found the answering machine tapes in Daphne's bedroom drawer. The tapes with the descriptions of Daphne, the details of the disappearance, talk of the tattoo and all the other messages that Agatha had been driving herself mad listening to. He had tried to dismiss his ideas that the girl had killed Kurt or had tried to poison Agatha – delusions, as the doctor had said, the likely effect of the thyroid.

But this tape was not the imagining of a delirious man, a man with a thyroid problem. This impostor had found the machine. Listened to the tapes, realised she vaguely resembled the girl. Learnt about the disappearance. Got a tattoo. Except she couldn't do anything about her limp.

Why? The girl was a mental case, no doubt had no parents of her own, was attracted by the chance to play happy families. She really was an invalid, this girl, and he would not expose her.

He wouldn't tell Agatha what he had discovered.

Sometimes, he knew, the truth may not be worth digging up.

Part Four

When the witch first came to Agatha Springs, she didn't yet know she was one.

This place was virgin bush, barely accessible by packhorses, strewn with stumps and rocks where men with the gleam of gold in their eyes wandered the trackless maze of mountain spurs that ran down the high country. Slopes rose steep and V-shaped on each side of the creek. The cemetery occupied the only flat land, a hundred metres up the sheer face. Bodies had to be hauled vertically to the cemetery. Everyone dreaded a funeral.

Nuggets were as common as currants in pudding. Grog shanties traded in gold dust, but soon the alluvial gold was stripped down to fifteen feet below.

I am twelve years old. Other girls knead bread, sew chaff bags for clothes. I collect tadpoles, put them in my jam jars to feed my fish, which I catch with a net in the creek.

I know already I want to swim underwater. I see how long I can hold my breath with the brown creek-water over my head. Under the water, I can't hear that ear-wrenching pounding of the gold mines at work.

'She'll drown herself.'

My mother. I like the worried look on her face when I eventually surface. My mother who runs *Agatha Springs*, the

161

smallest hotel in the world, where men who smell of alcohol invade what should be our home.

In winter when the water's too cold I lie down on the rocky bank of the creek and place my head under the water. I try to keep my eyes open and the water flows into my body, watering down my blood, making me feel part of the creek. I feel it flow into the strange folds behind my ears, the ones other girls do not have. The creek flowing into me. The creek flowing out to the sea. Away from this place.

Under the water, I touch sweet bliss, learn how to breathe like a fish.

The creek taught me how to control certain events. I can read other people's thoughts when my head is under the water. Or not exactly when it is under, because then it is too full of sweet bliss, but for a few hours afterwards, as if my mind has been washed clean. I start charging my friends a penny to see me do tricks.

Guess which colour they are thinking of.

Which number.

And I can also tell them which plant to eat to fix a stomach-ache. (I know by the smell of the plant.)

Eventually I teach myself how to go into the same trance without the water. And to fly cross-legged like yogis, like the old wizards on magic carpets – it's not true (as they would say later) that I use a broomstick. Most inelegant. No, a nice double-weave hand-loomed deep-blue-as-night Persian carpet suits me better.

Now I'm twenty-six and still unmarried.

Fussy, they say, and does not take enough care of her grooming, black hair sticking up everywhere like a witch. They even accuse me of being the werewolf who moans under the full moon at night, frightening the sinners.

I wear the clothes of the Chinese market gardeners on the outskirts of town – they are my friends. Black silk pants and a long satin over-dress of deep royal blue, which darken my pale eyes.

On Saturday nights at the hotel, I have a stage show. I read minds to warm them up, but my big number is in the fish-tank. I swim with the fish, underwater, holding my breath for longer than anyone can believe.

They do not know, of course, that behind my ears I have tiny but efficient gills.

I still live in the smallest hotel in the world, *Agatha Springs*, but I am in charge now and I do not take in guests.

I secretly give potions to the town's lovers, to the town's sick too, but only when the doctors have given up. The desperate come to me in secret but barely nod to me in the street when they are well again. But no one would dare to hurt me – all have been helped, or know someone I have helped. I know all the town's secret loves and spites and envies.

My best friends are the Chinese, who never need to come to me, having remedies of their own, and whose green lines of vegetables in precise, weedless rows cover the lowest slopes on the edge of town. If it weren't for the Chinese, no one would eat vegetables.

I show them my spells, bunches of sweet or evil herbs in little bags of hessian – they act on the soul, which knows how to breathe in scent. In return, they show me their magic – pickled things in jars – and how to burn joss sticks to communicate with ancestors. They call this the incense of the heart.

At first I think he is a handsome man. Very tall and thin with thick blond hair and a soft blond moustache. He comes from somewhere cold, Switzerland or Iceland, and his accent is very slight and sweet and his skin is the colour of milky tea. It would be smooth to touch, but there is something about a moustache, something fox-like, that makes me shudder.

I could go away with him, I think at first, as I watch him fuss with the sugar spoon for the first time, go away to wherever it is he comes from. Away from here.

He need not know the baby isn't his.

So I smile at him and let him steal a kiss in the shadowy hallway. (Or do I kiss him first? I have kissed at least a dozen men, I like it, on the mouth, soft and lingering.) Then he moves away.

'Eve was made from Adam's rib,' he says in an explanation I can't fathom.

I wonder why his lips are cold. But after that he is confident, asking me about what it is like here growing up among rough miners, doing tricks in the fish tank on Saturday nights with them all watching me.

He makes it sound a terrible place.

'And what about the werewolf that steals children that they talk about in the paper?'

'Oh, so there are werewolves in the Bible?' I ask, and he blushes. Bible people, after all, should not believe in werewolves (that is for us).

And he believes the Bible, word for word.

His aunt arrives one day and tells me, matter-of-factly, that she has arranged the marriage for Easter. In fact it is she who asks me to marry him. Perhaps that is the custom in Switzerland.

'You should jump at the chance,' she adds, allowing her eyes to sweep for a telling moment over my swelling belly. 'You're no longer young. And in your condition ... He is willing to take you on, as long as there is no more talk of spells or witchcraft.'

I listen to the delicate clink of her spoon on the china cup as she stirs in her sugar.

'And no more stage shows, making a spectacle of yourself.'

So he moved into my house with his aunt on our wedding day.

My tiny house is built high up on the side of the valley. The land slopes so much that you walk up steps from the gate to the front door, then halfway down the hallway there's another set of steps up to the back of the house. And out the back window, eight more steps, above which chooks roam, lopsided on the slope, and the herbs and vegetables rise off into a layer of cloud before the back fence. It is still planted with magic ingredients for my spells and strange herbs from China.

When it rained the water used to rush through the hall like a torrent. My husband has built a canal, V-shaped, which diverts the water around each side of the house to an underground barrel in front of it. Here, water stays cool, ready for summer, or overflows into the street. There is a magic spring too, next to the house, but my husband has built a bathroom over it. The water runs in taps now, but it is still tasty to drink, clear, and has a calming effect on me.

I make stained glass with a mermaid, who I think of as my unborn child, sitting by a waterfall. When she is born, she will sleep in this back room, looking out through the stained glass onto the garden at the back.

I sit in there, cross-legged like the Chinese, on the floor next to the crib I have got ready for her, and burn joss-sticks the way they have taught me. I say the prayers they have taught me. And my own spells. So that my daughter will always stay with me, in this house, in this room.

Because here, the garden and house can look after her.

We sit in front of the fireplace, the three of us, and I seek comfort in the earth floor with neat reed mats that I bought from the Chinese merchants, the gold brocade curtains, the Chinese lanterns. No one else grows vegetables here except me and the Chinese market gardeners. This gives me an excuse to visit them. They continue to give me strange seedlings and we swap magic recipes secretly.

I look at my husband. I no longer find him handsome – it must have been the novelty of the look of such a foreign man. He is a cold man in all ways – his skin, even his breath when he kisses my cheek goodnight. His hair is white-blond, not normal, and his eyes are so pale blue they look as if a film of white cloud lies over the colour.

He hates the sun and these gold-strewn hills, half-covered in cloud, are safe enough from it. He is a Bible kind of man and the three of us often drink tea and read scriptures together in the parlour, full now of Aunt's framed tapestries. Aunt and I have our tea black and strong, but he must have one and a half spoons of sugar and a little milk from the jug.

In the house now only holy books and books about nature are allowed. Desperate to relieve the new tedium of the life of a respectable woman, I find drama in a book called *The Life of The Bee* by Maurice Maeterlinck. I am in love with Maurice.

My favourite part is the massacre of the drones, as they wake to find death via the virgin females.

They wake, in pious wonder, they cannot believe their eyes; and their astonishment struggles through their sloth as a moonbeam through marshy water. They stare amazedly around them, convinced that they must be victims of some mistake ... they take a step towards the vats of honey to seek comfort there. But ended for them are the days of May honey, the wine-flower of lime-trees and fragrant ambrosia of thyme and sage, of marjoram and white clover. Where the path once lay open to the kindly, abundant reservoirs, that so invitingly offered their waxen and sugary mouths, there stands now a burning bush all alive with poisonous, bristling stings.

The atmosphere of the city is changed: in lieu of the friendly perfume of honey, the acrid odour of poison prevails; thousands of tiny drops glisten at the end of the stings, and diffuse rancour and hatred.

Truly, a drama. A story of revolution, debauchery and murder. My husband does not know this secret story of passion, hidden between the innocent covers of *The Life of Bees*. He thinks it is a manual to help me in the hive that I keep for honey, set outside in the garden. I read it over and over, even in front of him. He doesn't suspect. Just a nature book, he thinks. Other things I must keep more secret.

Imagine him finding me one night, when he comes unannounced, with all my Tarot cards spread out on the floor, my red candles, my little hessian spell-bags to call up the white angels … or sitting cross-legged in a trance, bathed in sweet bliss, breathing in the smoking, pluming, incense of the heart.

So now I live in Purgatory Road, with him.

I look at my carpet, lying quietly on the floor like any old carpet, but tacked down now just in case it gets ideas of its own.

He says he married me because of the baby, to save me from Satan, but I know it was because I have a house – he and his aunt had nothing. (My lover, where is he now, the boy with wild eyes and loving hands, who ran away as soon as he knew I was with child?)

I try to be grateful for what my husband calls his generous offer.

We sleep in separate beds.

We attend church together.

Gradually people stop asking me to help them.

Visitors stop coming, except from his church, and he is happy.

For twelve hours I scream, but no one hears me.

For twelve hours a day, in fact, nothing is heard above the roar of the stampers, the giant pumping heartbeat of the town, giving it life. When they stop, the quiet is unnerving, like a death.

It is winter, and the town is shrouded in fog and mist and rain, and my husband and his aunt sit outside rugged up on the damp veranda.

They do not want to hear me scream as I try to push the baby out.

The baby is born with one foot shaped like a fishtail. They will not let me hold her.

'The mark of faeries,' he says. 'She is a changeling.'

'You should not have married him. What I wanted for him was a normal life,' cries his Aunt.

I scream to hold the baby in my arms, but my husband takes her away, will not let me hold her. I am too weak to move.

Hours later, the Aunt comes in and announces that the baby is dead.

Already buried.

Rain falls, gushing down each side of the house, and we listen to it. I still cannot move, and wonder if I am already dead, lying in my bed, as my husband sits by me in a straight-backed chair.

He tries to read my face, but it is the face of a professional performer, a Saturday Night Magician. It is blank. But I am broken.

I know he has killed her.

He will pay.

A baby who dies like that cannot ascend to the Golden Realm, cannot give up this world because she has not lived. She must play with the faeries, between both worlds, watching, waiting for her chance to come back again to the earth, to rid herself of her pain. I know she will come back to this house, this garden, her room with the stained-glass windows.

So I declared a wake for the baby, at which I served a feast. I served my husband and his aunt with a salad of hemlock, a soup of onion and narcissus bulbs, followed by a cake of pressed castor beans mixed with linseed. I poisoned them both.

After which, I dug up the baby. Stripped her to the skin and anointed her with sticky earth on which I placed gold dust so that she was completely covered, especially her dear fish-tailed foot, beautiful to me.

I ride the long way to the magic place on horseback. It takes a whole day to reach it.

I take the baby down to the grassy knoll. Down by the magic creek at midnight. The grass is unnaturally green here, a magic circle, and under the stones of the fireplace I have built there, I store my magic spells, away from prying eyes. I burn the incense of the heart; I teach the dead baby all I know, all she will need to come back to earth one day.

Then I place her on a raft heaped with gold and emeralds, for her to offer to the goddess so that she may return to earth, seek her revenge again and again against the man who killed her until she finds peace.

As the raft leaves the shore of the creek, I hear music with trumpets, flutes and singing which shakes the mountains and valleys until the raft reaches the centre of the creek. Then I watch it slowly sink into the muddy water.

I know that, like me, my baby cannot drown.

The story spread, and was transformed, about the golden child. Some said it was not a child, but a nugget of gold that was thrown into the creek, a nugget shaped like a child. They called it Golden Child Walk. They said a witch had ridden on horseback with a dead child, down to the green magic circle by the creek.

The night the baby was given its golden rite, a thicket of blackberries grew up around the house.

Alone now in the empty house, the witch lived on.

And on.

She sculpted a dragon from white stone, placed it in the garden over the outlet of the underground spring to protect the garden until the return of her child.

Magpies arrived and sat on the dragon's curled tongue – in a blink, they disappeared. Swallowed whole. Around the dragon grew a circle of thick green grass and red-capped toadstools. As the witch grew older, weaker, blackberries started taking over the rest of the garden, but dared not encroach on the dragon's territory. On nights of the full moon red blood oozed from the dragon's mouth.

Magpies drank it and grew as big as eagles. Magpies swarmed over the blackberry buried house at dawn and dusk, screeching. They had seen the house split in two by the man and the woman screaming inside it. They had watched him come outside carrying a newborn child. Too still.

Later they had watched her mount her horse, carry the bundle to the creek.

They had seen the baby glitter gold, as the raft left the shore.

Outside the Golden Realm she would wait with the faeries until she saw a girl, at that time between childhood and womanhood, that very split second, that moment when a mother no longer recognises her child, the time of separation, the time the child looks at her mother, ever so briefly, and the mother sees the eyes of a stranger. Assessing her. For in that split second, during that rapid metamorphosis, a faery can enter the soul of the girl.

But once incarnate, her blood, forced around her body, into her heart, out again, would hurt her. She would learn ways to rid herself of the constant pain (she would not know that all faeries feel this ache of gravity when they assume mortal form, with its human blood which drags them down to earth from where they wait outside the Golden Realm) when she returned to this place of poison and honey.

The End

Also Available from BeWrite Books

www.bewrite.net

Back There
by Howard Waldman

Harry Grossman sees his world through the viewfinder of a battered camera. And he photographs it all, from the peeling posters and graffiti on grubby city walls to the most intimate moments of his mysterious French sweetheart. He becomes a permanent guest at her family's ramshackle country cottage, thirty miles and a century away from modern Paris. Harry, the New York outsider, calls it paradise and photographs the Model T Ford on the roof, the archaic well and scythe, the top-secret wild mushroom spots, and the reluctant Lauriers themselves.

They assume that outsider Harry will soon be a member of the family, but the strange photographer with his growing mountain of prints and negatives and imperfect French is not a man for snap decisions. Aren't things already perfect in this paradise? Someone once said, though, that the only paradises are lost paradises.

Back There is a touching and powerfully nostalgic transatlantic love story, sometimes verging on the comic, sometimes on the tragic. France and the French, too often caricatures of their own special reality, are presented with absolute authenticity.

With soft-focus subtlety, Howard Waldman shows that Europe and America are two continents divided by a perceived common culture of art and love - and that light-years separate Paris and Manhattan and the lives and values of the Lauriers and the Grossmans.
Paperback ISBN 1-904492-88-6

Redemption of Quapaw Mountain
by Bertha Sutliff

When mountain man Beaver Mosely builds a log cabin on Blue Meadow for his bride, Keziah, it looks like the new 20th Century holds nothing but promise.

But that is before the newlyweds discover that their land is cursed - stained by the blood of an innocent Indian tribe and haunted by the ghosts of a secret and shameful past.

Bertha Sutliff brings back to life the isolated Arkansas highlands of the early 1900s and their unique people, culture and mythology in a sweeping saga of struggle and hope, love and hate, life and death ...
Paperback ISBN 1-904492-38-X

Whispers of Ghosts
by Ron McLachlan

Up here, forget everything you thought you knew about the weather. On this mysterious yet enchanting island strange things can happen: omens, magic, restless spirits ploughing the night on their endless quest for peace, the very land and sea can speak to you of secrets, and of their very own character. When you leave, the dull ache of longing will claw in your heart drawing you back. It's a place like no other. The Isle of Arnasay.

Three generations of the Waters clan lie at the centre of this powerful tale about what happens when families and communities fall apart.

Told through the eyes of Madeline, from twenty years in the future, by which time she has become a successful, Manhattan-dwelling novelist, we are transported on a roller-coaster-like emotional voyage through the Sea Kingdoms of the Hebrides.

Steeped in Celtic, Viking, and Pictish cultural heritage, this gripping novel of close-knit family and community dynamics tells how these forces come into play and wreak havoc with the lives of the Hebrides islanders.

This tale will have meanings, echoing the harsh realities of island life, for all Gaels, at home and abroad. But its appeal goes much wider than that. You can't choose your family; all too often you can't choose your friends either. Sometimes, you can't tell the difference.

Paperback ISBN 1-904492-62-2

The Stones of Petronicus
by Peter Tomlinson

A new-born baby is left naked and exposed to die on a city wall while his father is hanged for petty theft a few feet away amid the cheers and hoots of a crazed mob.

Petronicus, an itinerant healer and man of wisdom, takes the babe to heart and together they begin a quest for knowledge, groping through a maze of magic and madness to find answers in the cruel and mysterious ancient world.

The boy grows to manhood in strange lands where a chosen few risk death in their search for truth, bitterly opposed by ruthless rulers and puppet priests who strive to enslave their subjects in a perpetual Dark Age of superstition and suspicion.

The heart-warming, honest but complex simplicity Petronicus and his adopted son share leave the reader wiser than when he joined them on their remarkable journey.

Not since the Fables of Aesop has a book like this been written. And Tomlinson wraps the sage advices in the tales Petronicus tells in a story as intriguing and exciting as any high-octane thriller - with characters so real you'll meet them time and again in your dreams ... and your nightmares.

Paperback ISBN 1-904492-76-2

Printed in the United Kingdom
by Lightning Source UK Ltd.
108477UKS00001B/136

9 781905 202126